MUSCLE
FOR THE
WING

A RINEHART SUSPENSE NOVEL

A RINEHART SUSPENSE NOVEL

MUSCLE FOR THE WING

DANIEL WOODRELL

HENRY HOLT AND COMPANY   NEW YORK

Library of Congress Cataloging-in-Publication Data
Woodrell, Daniel.
Muscle for the wing.
(A Rinehart suspense novel)
I. Title.
PS3573.06263M87   1988   813'.54   88-9134
ISBN 0-8050-0788-1

First Edition

Designed by Katy Riegel with Abby Kagan
Printed in the United States of America
1 3 5 7 9 10 8 6 4 2

ISBN 0-8050-0788-1

Why, a human being should be the most fabulous creature of all, which is the way the Man Upstairs intended when He put the show on the road in the first place. But what happens is, one human gets to plotting with another human and maybe another and another, and after a while they all decide to be generals. So right away they form a combine in order to get the Hungarian lock on the mooches and the suckers, and that kind of action touches off all the war jolts from here to Zanzibar. That's human endeavor for you.

—MINNESOTA FATS

MUSCLE
FOR THE
WING

A RINEHART SUSPENSE NOVEL

1

Wishing to avoid any risk of a snub at The Hushed Hill Country Club, the first thing Emil Jadick shoved through the door was double-barreled and loaded. He and the other two Wingmen were inappropriately attired in camouflage shirts and ski masks, but the gusto with which they flaunted their firearms squelched any snide comments from the guests seated around the poker table.

Jadick took charge of the rip-off by placing both cool barrels against the neck of a finely coiffed, silver-haired gent, and saying loudly, "Do I have your attention? We're robbin' you assholes—any objections?"

The table was a swank walnut octagon, with drink wells and stacks of the ready green on a blue felt top. The gentlemen who had assembled around it for an evening of high-stakes Hold 'Em were well dressed, well fed, and well heeled, but now their mouths hung loose and their poolside tans paled.

"Hands on the table, guys," Jadick said. "And don't any of you act one-armed." A short man with an air of compact power, Jadick moved with brisk precision and spoke calmly. He pulled back the hammers on his archaic but awesome weapon and said, "Scoop the fuckin' manna, boys."

"Check," said Dean Pugh. He and Cecil Byrne, his fellow Wingman, went slowly around the table shoving wads of cash into a gym bag that had St. Bruno High Pirates stenciled on the side.

Twelve hands were palm-down on the blue felt. Manicured fingers twitched in obvious attempts to covertly twist wedding bands and pinkie rings so that the flashy side was down.

Jadick watched the fingers and rings business until two or three had indeed been twisted into seeming insignificance, and the owners began to relax. He then said, "Get all the jewelry, too."

"Check," said Pugh, a daffy man who oddly relished the orderliness of military jargon.

Pugh and Byrne both carried darkly stylish pistols, and as they went around the table they pressed them to the ears of the players. While they raked up the money and jerked fine gems from plump fingers, Jadick scanned the room, nodding his head at how closely it resembled what he had expected. Tournament trophies and low-round medals were enclosed in a huge glass case, along with antique wooden-shafted clubs and other golfing memorabilia. A long horseshoe bar of richly hued wood halved the room and several conference tables were dotted about the other side. Just beyond the poker table, nailed at a dominating height on the wall, there were scads of stern portraits, presumably of the exclusionary but sporty founders.

"Hah!" Jadick snorted. Some long-festering desire took hold of him and he shoved the shotgun against the neck of the privileged man before him until he was rudely rubbing an upscale face against the tabletop. "I bet all of you sell city real estate to niggers and live in the 'burbs—am I right?"

One of the wide-eyed, harkening faces turned to Jadick. This man was younger than the other players, with a big bottle of Rebel Yell in front of him and an empty spot where his small heap of money had been. His hair was closely cropped and blond and his cheeks were full and flushed.

"Your accent," he said, "it ain't from around here. It's northern. That's why you don't know you're makin' a mistake, man—this is a protected game."

"Really?" Jadick said. "If this is '*protected*,' I'm goin' to get over real good down here."

Despite the low hum of air-conditioning, the victims sweated gushingly and shook with concern, for, not only were they being shorn of their gambling money, but history was staggering and order decaying before their eyes. The swinging side of the St. Bruno night world had been run as smoothly and nearly as openly as a pizza franchise for most of a decade and now these tourists from the wrong side of the road somewhere else were demonstrating the folly of such complacence. Auguste Beaurain, the wizened little genius of regional adoration, had run the upriver dagos, the downriver riffraff, the homegrown Carpenter brothers, and the out-of-state Dixie Mafia from this town and all its profitable games in such an efficient and terrifying manner that no one had truly believed he would ever again be tested this side of the pearly gates.

But here and now these strangers, too ignorant of local folklore to know how much danger they were in, were taking the test and deciding on their own grades.

"I think we should make 'em drop trou," Pugh said. He widened an eyehole in his ski mask with a finger from his gun-free hand. "These are the sort of hick sharpies who figure money belts are real nifty."

Jadick nodded and stepped back so that he had a clear shot at all concerned.

"A fine notion," he said. He raised the barrel up and down. "You heard him, dudes—stand up and strip." Jadick added scornfully, "Don't be shy."

At this coupling of humiliation with monetary loss, there were some sighs and whimpers. But all of the men stood and unbuckled their pants; then, five of the six dropped them to their ankles.

"What'd I say?" Pugh said. "There's a money belt." Pugh advanced on the man with the thick white money belt and pulled on it and it stretched like a big fish story. "What the hell?"

"Man," said the shamefaced tubby, as the released elastic snapped back, "man, it's a corset. Over the winter I got fat."

"Shit," Pugh said, then noticed that the blond man who'd earlier yammered about "protected games" had yet to bare his butt to financial scrutiny. "Say, Jim," he said harshly, "take 'em down!"

"Come on," Cecil said, "I got the dough—let's cut."

"Not 'til this guy does what I said. He's holdin' out."

The blond man's face was red and wet. Fear was wringing his features like a sink-washed sock. He was too jammed up to make a definite response: he looked from one face to another; studied his feet; blinked rapidly; then said: "This is a protected game. I'm telling you all . . ."

"Shut up, Gerry," the corseted man said. "If you'd been at the door like . . ."

Jadick rapped the shotgun barrel on the table.

"He's the guard," he said. "Get his piece."

But as that final sentence was still being uttered, the blond, with one hand holding his unbuckled trousers, slid the other hand behind his back where holsters clipped on, and began to spin away, grunting and sucking for air.

Pugh screamed, "Yeah, right!," then cut him down before his pistol cleared his shirttails, spotting his shots, tearing the man open in the belly, the thigh, one wrist and, finally, just above the left ear.

The body slumped against the wall in an acutely angled posture that nothing alive could withstand. Blood pumped up out of the wrist onto the wall, and instantly washed down in a wide smear.

"Anybody else?" Pugh asked, expecting, as a response, silence, which he received. The Jockey-shorted high rollers were immobilized by the noise, the blood, and the lingering scent of gunfire.

"Hit the door," Jadick said gruffly. He used the gun barrel to point the way. "Let's go." He was not upset that murder had been required, for, in the short run, the only run that really mattered, it might set a useful precedent. Yeah, the hicks will know that some new rough element has dropped in on their town. "I'll be right behind."

Pugh and Byrne backed through the door while Jadick acted as rear guard. He looked out of the Chinese-shaped eyeholes and saw so many of the things he'd never liked reflected in these tony, awestruck, half-dressed money-bag types that he couldn't pass up a chance at scot-free revenge. The silver-haired man whose neck he'd used for a gun rest was at a handy remove so he hopped forward and chopped blue steel across his fine, blue-chip nose, heard the crack and quash and knew the gent would now have a common Twelfth Street beak he would be ribbed about on the nineteenth hole from here 'til the grave. With considerable satisfaction he watched the dude sink to his knees, torrents of red ruining his tasteful silk knit ensemble. He did a little swivel, flourishing that ominous piece, and all of the men went belly-down on the carpet with their hands uselessly over their heads, and Jadick, as a signature of his scorn, blasted the fancy tabletop, scattering cards and whiskey-sour glasses, a liter of Rebel Yell, a pint of Maalox, and the thoughts of all those prone below him. The blue felt was tufted and ripped and unsuitable for any more games, and Jadick, as he left, said, "The universe owes me plenty, motherfuckers, and I aim to collect!"

2

Paradise might be a setup like this, Shade thought as he swiveled on his barstool. That is, if paradise turned out to be a long, narrow tavern on the near northside of a grumpy downriver town, that attracted a primarily female clientele who packed the joint to drink and gossip, smoke and be seen but not picked up. The place never echoed with come-on lines, and unescorted males were not encouraged to hang around. Beauticians, secretaries, a lawyer or two, frazzled housewives, and sorefooted hustling gals sat on the stuffed chairs and bamboo thrones lined along the walls, their drinks on small white side tables. Many thumbed through copies of *Vogue, True Romance, Sports Illustrated,* and *People* that were left in stacks on the corners of the black bar. A sign above the pyramid of wineglasses behind the counter said, MAGGIE'S KEYHOLE, LADIES WELCOME.

Jazz from more romantic days played on a tape machine and came swinging sweetly from speakers hung below the ceiling. Feet shod in high heels and flat heels, cowgirl boots and tennies tapped the polished wood floor unconsciously but in perfect time with Sidney Bechet or Johnny Hodges, Fletcher Henderson, the Duke, the Count, the Hawk or the Prez.

Shade, one of only three males in the room, was diverted from his smiling surveillance when the bartendress, Nicole Webb, said, "See anything interesting, Rene?"

"Oh," he said beatifically, "it's *all* interesting."

"Is that so," Nicole said. "You pick the ones you like, point 'em out, and I'll be glad to make the introductions for you, there, stud."

"That's a very modern offer," Shade said as he turned to face her across the bar. "But I'm just here waiting on you, Nic."

Nicole was on the perky side of thirty and had wild, tumbling cascades of black hair that hung to her ribs and had never been quite brushed into submission. Her eyes were green and widely spaced on her thin, sharp-chinned face, giving her a vaguely vulpine expression. She was tanned and tall, with no slack on her at all. Every move she made gave an impression of cultivated energy. Though it was the baseball season she wore a red basketball tank top with blue lettering across the front that read, Maggie's Keyhole Peepers.

"Well, why don't you look at *me*, once in a while?" she asked.

Shade tapped his empty glass, shrugged, then said, "If you'd bend over more, I would."

Nicole pulled herself straight, arched her spine, theatrically jutted her rear, then slid a hand over her tight denimed haunch.

"Nice stuff, huh, buster?"

"You know it," Shade answered. "Private stock."

"That's odd," she said as her posture folded back to

normal and she removed the empty glass. "The Culligan Man always says the same thing. You two ought to meet." She put the glass in the sink, dried her hands and pulled out a deck of cards. "One hand for the next drink, okay?" "Deal 'em." Shade won three hands in a row and demonstrated his recent conversion to cocktails rather than neat slugs of rum by ordering a manhattan, a vodka martini, and a sidecar. "I'm on a roll, which is maybe good, or bad. My gut doesn't know yet."

As Nicole dealt the blackjack hands Maggie Gallant came in from the back room and stood behind her. Though Maggie was well into her seventies, her hair was still colored in a dark hue so vigorously youthful that only vain old dames or presidents would try to pass it off as natural. She wore, as usual, a floor-length black outfit that hid her wide beam and gnarled legs and gave her a serious presence.

She looked at the cards and said to Nicole, "Take a hit, honey."

"On seventeen, Mag?"

"Take a hit."

Nicole did so, and when the down cards were flipped found she had bested Shade's pat nineteen with a long-shot three.

"Hah, hah," Maggie said, stating a laugh but not having one. "Don't try that with your own money, honey."

"My streak is ended," Shade said. "I guess I'll actually *buy* a beer now." He put a dollar on the bar and Nicole pulled a draw, then slid the mug to him. "Bois-sec," he said, raised the beer and took a swallow.

Maggie tapped one of her sharp-nailed fingers on his forearm, snagging his attention. "So, Diamond Jim," she said in her low raspy voice, "I heard you're gonna take my gal here up into the woods somewhere and make her sleep on the ground, in the mud where snakes crawl. I heard you're callin' it a vacation."

"It's a fishing trip, Maggie."

"You have to sleep on the dirt in the woods to go fishin'?"

"That's part of the experience."

Maggie shook her head and sighed with something akin to disdain.

"It figures," she said. "You cops are the cheapest fuckers I ever met. Any two-bit horse player'd at least take her to the Biloxi Beach and put her up at a Motel Six."

"Right," Shade said. "And charge it all on a stolen credit card."

"So? What kind of a cop are you who can't scare up an extra buck for vacation?"

"A more or less straight one, Mag."

"Oh, I get it," she said with raised brows, "you think that'll help you someday."

"Naw, Mag, I'm cute but not stupid." He drank some more beer and smiled. "I'll make her a bed of pine needles and feed her rainbow trout grilled fresh from the stream."

"That part sounds fine," Nicole said. "But I've gone fishing with you before and I've never seen you actually *catch* a fish."

"I will up in the Ouachitas," he said. Shade was about sixty stitches past good-looking, with pale nicks around his eyes and a high-bridged nose that had been counterpunched level lower down. His blue eyes were suggestive of heat and doggedness, and the trimness of his body indicated physical discipline. His hair was long, brown, and weeded out slightly on top. Though he had lately begun to yearn to cast a more dashing silhouette, he still dressed like a laid-off longshoreman, favoring tight, dark T-shirts and khaki slacks, no socks and white, slip-on deck shoes. "From what I read in the paper, the trout up in the Ouachitas are practically gangstomping unwary anglers."

"How exciting," Maggie said. "I think you can buy 'em tamed and frozen at Kroger's. It's not even that far of a drive."

A Johnny Hodges version of "Don't Get Around Much Anymore" was lilting from the speakers, and the miscellaneous hullabaloo of the tavern merged with the jaunty sax to make a pleasant racket. Two women sitting on a short couch near the bar seriously debated the merits of Krystle and Alexis, while another audible pair clanged empty beer pitchers and said, "*Home*-ward! *Home*-ward!*"

"Aw," Shade said, "listen, up there it's another world. That's what I want on my vacation. I don't want a beach version of St. Bruno. I want another world for five days. The river up there, it's not the color of shoe leather like this one here. Huh-uh. It's clearer'n baby piss and cooler'n Duke Ellington. You drop in a six-pack and in ten minutes you got the perfect beer." He emptied his own mug of brew. "I got a pup tent, too, you know. For comfort."

Shade's conception of comfort, trotted out so baldly, caused a pause in the badinage, the two women looking on him with the same sort of worldly pity that a claim of actually preferring store-bought biscuits over those made from scratch would have drawn. Their unsmiling but tender stares masked the little voices in their heads that said, "Son, you are not to be trusted on matters of taste. But to tell you would be too sad."

For his part Shade was transported between his ears,

already several hours away by car, in the middle of a brisk, chill stream of modest depth, sniffing the abundance of mountainside pines, using ancient angling cunning to con a few fillets from that old bumpkin, Mother Nature. He would watch for the eagles known to be there, in the highest parts of that rugged geography, always ready to be awed by a glimpse of the elegant floating predator, the swooping national symbol.

"Did I tell you they've got eagles up there?" he asked. When no one seemed to have heard him he said in a louder voice, "Hey, give me another beer."

Shade watched as saucy Nicole, the longest-running romance of his adult life, her arms and shoulders bare in the hoop top, went to the tap and pulled back the spigot, the movement raising her left arm, offering him a tantalizing view of her pit hair which she never shaved, a fashion touch she'd adopted at nineteen while spending a year in Trieste pretending to be a Euro-peasant. As she brought his mug toward him he watched the familiar, slight wobbling of her endearing, pert little tits, and found himself suddenly flashing on sweaty, naked scenes in a soft bed.

"When is Maggie going to let you off, Nic?"

She set the beer on a square pad in front of him.

"Oh, Carol should be here in a few minutes. At midnight. Mags'll let me leave then." She put her elbows on the bar and rested her chin in her palms, her face close to his. "Baby, you're getting a little red around the eyes."

"It's those cocktails," Shade said. "I should stick with what I know."

Near the door a clutch of white-haired gals called out, "Yoo-hoo, dearie—we need more of that sour-mash tea, please."

12

As Nicole headed off to wait on them she said from the side of her mouth, "Just don't drink yourself useless."

Maggie rejoined Shade, a can of diet Dr Pepper in her hands.

"I'm holdin' some dough for you," she said.

"I know."

"You want to cash it in or let it ride on something?"

"There can't be much," he said.

"Thirty-five measly dollars," Maggie said. "I wouldn't even bother to handle your chickenshit bets if I didn't like you." She sipped her soda, hardly taking enough to swallow. "Less my ten percent and you got thirty-one fifty."

"Ooh, I'm rich," Shade said in a flat tone, "but I'll risk it all."

"I *adore* you sporty cops. Who're you takin'?"

Half lit and feeling expansive behind that recent flash of carnal expectations, Shade said, "The trustee at the nut house gave me a tip, Mag. Those crazies are so wired to the unseen I'm going to take it, too. Whoever's going against the Atlanta Braves gets my nod. And let it roll like that day by day 'til I lose, or own this joint, okay?"

"Whatever you say, mon petit chou." She placed her hand over his. "But that's sort of a wild bet for you."

"Aw," Shade said, "I'm trying to build up my retirement fund."

For the next several minutes Shade kept his whistle wet and watched as Nicole marched up and down the narrow room, carrying pitchers of beer and margaritas to the needy. Finally there was a respite when everybody had a drink and she came and stood behind the bar at his end of the rail.

"Whew," she said, "it's midnight—where's Carol?"

"Wish I knew."

13

A second later a pair of hands slapped down on the bar.

"Hey, Nicole," the young woman said, "how you doin'?"

"All right, Wanda. How 'bout yourself?"

"Aw, the normal. Give me two sixes of Jax in a sack, will you?"

"Sure."

Shade always checked out anybody named Lulu, Candy, Dixie or Wanda, so he did a quick scan: a young gal of about the old voting age with hair of that eye-catching, burnt-red color that spelled trouble in pulp paperbacks, a short, juicy build with an abundance of feminine bounce and a feisty freckled face that dared you to make something of it.

As the sack of beer was laid out Wanda pushed a bill across the wood. When she pocketed the change she picked up the bag and said, "Be seein' you, Nic."

"Not for a while," Nicole said.

"Oh, yeah? Why is that?"

"Rene, here," Nicole said, pointing her head toward him, "is taking me on a fishing trip tomorrow. We're going to sleep outside on the dirt—like the homeless."

"That's men for you," Wanda said and favored Shade with an unfavorable glance. "They always expect *you* to sleep on whatever hard ground *they* picked out." She then turned back to Nicole and smiled. "Have as much fun as he'll let you."

After Wanda was out the door Shade asked, "Who is she?"

"Just a Frogtown girl," Nicole answered. "Tough kid. Plays on The Peepers basketball team. Rugged little heartbreaker, too—flings elbows all over and led the team in rebounds from the guard spot."

"I guess I don't know her."

"Well, her name used to be Wanda Bone, but she's married now. It's Bouvier, I think. Something like that."

"I know a couple of Bouviers," Shade said. "But not the young ones."

Nicole looked at the clock, then at the door, hoping to see Carol.

"Well, the one she married is a lot older'n her," she said. She took a sip of Shade's beer. "He's older'n you."

"Could it be Ronnie Bouvier?"

"Yeah, I think so. I think that's him."

"Ronnie's in the joint."

"Yeah, life's a bitch," Nicole said. There were other things on her mind. "If Carol doesn't show pretty quick I'm going to send you out to find her."

Well, just at that moment huffing Carol came in the back door, carrying her shoes. Nicole huddled with her briefly to hear the latest excuse, for Carol generally excelled at them, but this time she told the lame one about the dead car battery and the long dutiful walk in the midnight hour. In any case she took Nicole's place behind the bar.

After telling Maggie they'd be on the road at dawn and back next week, Shade and Nicole made it out of the bar and into the pleasant shirt-sleeve weather of a late summer night in the delta.

"So," Nicole said, "what's the plan?"

"Don't need one," Shade answered cryptically. "The rest of tonight is preordained, Miss Nastiness."

"How's that?"

"I read my horoscope this morning," Shade whispered as he pulled her close, slipping the straps of her tank top down and cupping a bared breast. "It was spelled out."

They made it to his car behind the bar and leaned

against it, doing some sloppy tongue weaving there beneath a dim streetlight.

"Uh-huh," Nicole said, "I'll bite—what'd your horoscope say?"

"It said, and I think it's true, that I should fellow you tonight and sex you down."

"Oh, that's all?" Nicole pulled her shirt all the way to her waist and clasped her hands above her head. "It didn't say where?"

"Baby, the stars left that up to you."

3

Wanda Bone Bouvier had that thing that makes a hound leap against his cage. It was a quality that was partly a bonus from nature and partly learned from cheesecake calendars and Tanya Tucker albums. Wanda had realized early on that her body was a taunt that sent would-be Romeos off on quests for Love Oil and ceiling mirrors and nerve. She had gone clean up to her sixteenth year, wandering school halls and pool halls, public parks and private parties, doing an earthy shimmy and sashay through them all. Though she had a deadpan gaze she had always sharply noted the weak knees and lolling tongues around her. She had found this effect to be delightful and fun until that fateful sixteenth year when she had gone with a girl friend to a roller-skating rink at dusk, and left before midnight in love forever with a fortyish gangster.

And, though this fine love had turned her around, and once or twice out, it had not turned suitors away. Her butt got pinched more than a baby's nose and even her snappy slaps back couldn't stop them. Since Ronnie had gone away to the Braxton Federal Pen she had come to feel like she was a go-go girl in strange men's dreams, for so many of them called or stopped her on the street to say they'd been thinking of her, constantly.

When Wanda parked in the drive of the drafty hulk of a house she'd been reduced to by jail widowhood, one of the more harmless of her trailing pack came across the street from the only other nearby house, and said, "I got off early, Wanda. Can I carry the sack?"

"That's okay, Leon," she said. She hoisted the sack and held it with both hands. "I'm tired tonight, but I can carry a little beer."

Leon Roe was a couple of years Wanda's elder, and he worked at a bump-and-grind place called Rio, Rio as a combination disc jockey—emcee. The man's sad slouch kept him under six feet tall. He was thin, with brown spit curls drooling down his forehead, and he wore a black coat with narrow lapels, a white shirt and a string tie, all in accordance with the resurging style of the rockabilly bad boy.

"When are you gonna take a lunch with me?" he asked, using a phrase that was meant to demonstrate that though he was on the bottommost rung of the showbiz ladder, he knew the lingo.

"Oh, are we goin' through this again?" Wanda said. "I always reserve the right to do whatever turns me on, Leon. And takin' a lunch with you ain't it."

Leon looked down at his boots, then up at the trees that swayed gently in the murky night.

"You know," he said, "it's totally dark out here."

"Don't even think about it," Wanda said firmly. "Look, you're an okay fella but not my sort. That's all. But if you think that because it's dark out here you got any chance of doin' somethin', you just forget it."

"I think you're the most beautiful girl in Frogtown," he said.

"Yeah, you've said that before, Leon. It won't get you anywhere." Wanda started up the dirt rut to the house, the sack of brew rustling in her arms. "See you later, Leon. Don't be mad."

When she reached the front door she looked over her shoulder and saw her only neighbor going back across the street to his house. Once inside she started turning on lamps in all the rooms, a nightly exorcism of fears she kept to herself. For, living out here past the railroad bridge, beyond the comforting reach of family and streetlights, Wanda survived cheaply but nervously. Vache Bayou, an offshoot of the Marais du Croche, was less than a free-throw toss behind the house. Being alone in this remote stretch of Frogtown, a section of the city where folks who thought they were tough got plenty of chances to prove it, left her feeling vulnerable to any number of the sneaky vicissitudes.

After a hot shower Wanda took a Baggie of home grown wacky-backy from the vegetable crisper in the fridge and sat at the kitchen table to twist a few sticks while letting the warm air dry her damp body.

A few minutes later she felt dry so she lit a joint and padded into the back room and turned on the stereo. As she listened to Roseanne Cash sing of people who could just about be her, Wanda dressed. She slipped on a sky-blue camisole with a ragged hem that reached to the bottom of her ribs, then pulled on a pair of shiny white satin shorts that seemed wetted onto her ass like hot breath on a cold jewelry window.

On her way through the kitchen she grabbed a Jax and went out to the screened-in back porch that overlooked the vast gumbo known as the bayou. She had left the arm up on the stereo so the album played over and over, and as she listened she pondered the regular things, the things she'd been pondering for the twenty-two months that Ronnie Bouvier had been in stir. Tonight she mainly contemplated what he'd asked her to do; that worried her the most by far, because she was already doing it. She loved him and she would do what needed to be done, as she always had. And to think that once upon a time, really just twenty-two months ago, he had seemed in possession of the answer to every important question in her life. But now *she* was expected to take care of *him* and get him out of Braxton with his future wrapped up and waiting pretty as a gift.

Oh, it was a spring night only five years before when she'd gone roller skating, a girl with a grown-up bod and an undeniable naughty rep, only to have Ronnie Bouvier, his black hair slicked back like a singer, pull up in a blue Corvette, idling alongside her at the Dairy Maid next to the rink. The first thing he'd said to her audible over the rumble of the powerful motor, was, "Those your tits, darlin'? They look like a movie star's tits to me." And she said back to him, "Well, I never," but truly she had, and in what seemed no more than a blink this man who was actually older than her father worked a romantic smash-and-grab on her, right there next to the skating rink, big-timing her out of her hip huggers before they even left the parking lot. She had instantly understood that he was different, and that this clothes-off grunting and pumping was the sweaty way of love. Two days later she moved out of her parents' house and into a brand-new world of sit-down restaurants, late nights in roadhouse back rooms, and money. Plenty of money. Then one day Ronnie told her the news that bad luck had been circling his block his whole life long and once again it had found a parking space right outside his door. It was a little federal thing Mr. B. set him up for, he explained, and it sounded worse than it was, so don't fret.

One week before beginning his sentence they were married legal at city hall.

Wanda heard the front door open but did not rise from her chair. She stared out through the screen, into the black and noisy bayou night. Her inhalations made the joint beam in the dark, and then the music died, and over the beep of bullfrogs she heard not one person, but a few, coming through the kitchen toward her.

The clopping feet stopped and she turned to see three men, backlit by the kitchen light, staring down at her.

"Emil," she said in a tone stoned flat, "you're supposed to come alone."

"I knew that," Jadick said. He came onto the porch and sat on the wide arm of her ratty old chair. He plucked the joint from her lips and took a hit. "I wanted to come alone, pun-kin, but we got ourselves a slight problem."

"Oh, yeah?"

"Yeah. Dean, here, killed a dude at the country club."

"Tell me you're lyin'."

"It ain't no lie."

"Oh, man," Wanda said. "Oh, man."

"He had to do it, Wanda. The dude did a no-no. He went for his piece. You understand we couldn't allow that."

Wanda raised her feet to the wide windowsill, crossed them, then leaned way back in the chair and kept her eyes

21

fixed on some unclear thing out there in the nightbog that had her mesmerized.

"I sure am glad I'm ripped," she said. "There's beer in the fridge. Help yourselves."

Later, Dean Pugh came out of the bathroom and stood in the hall, rubbing his skinny butt with both hands, and said, "I feel like I shit a hungry kitty!" After this unprovoked announcement he took a seat at the kitchen table, joining the others. "I want you to know," he said straight at Wanda, "that I hated killin' a white guy."

"Uh-huh," Wanda responded. Her eyes matched the shade of her hair now. Another half-smoked joint was dried to her lower lip and bobbed as she spoke, the cold ashes fluttering down. "I don't think they'll let you hide behind that, though. *Not legally.*"

"Well, I done hid behind a mask, lady, and it worked just fine."

Wanda had already listened to the whole dingy tale twice. The victim, "just another golfer type," was clearly dead, definitely in the processing department of Hell even now, the stolen getaway car had been left in an unpopulated part of Frogtown, and while they'd driven the clean car from there to here, the death gun had been pitched into the bayou. It hadn't seemed smart to be driving around town late at night after a robbery-murder so they would lay up here until it felt like time to leave. Probably by midday they'd cut out and get upriver to the deep swamp cabin they'd intended to stay in, and wouldn't be back until she'd cased the next job.

"Auguste's goin' to be awful mad," she said somberly. "That's a scary event, too, when *he* loses his temper."

"Fuck him," Jadick said. "Let him run all over bein'

22

mad—that's what we want. That's what *Ronnie* wants."
Jadick smoothly sucked off half a can of brew. "When us
guys have got it set up and Ronnie and them other Wingmen get out, why, bein' mad at us will be a mistake."

Finally noticing the dead roach dangling from her
mouth, Wanda spit it onto the tabletop.

"I don't know," she said. "I don't know about doin'
any more of this if you all're goin' to waste people. That
might be the wrong gimmick for around here."

"Bullshit," said Dean, hotly. Cecil, wraithlike Cecil,
watched him with admiring eyes. "Listen up to me, girl.
We got a schedule, a plan, a design for The Wing." He
pointed at her face and his own bony visage scowled.
"Now, Ronnie won't be happy if you wuss out on us, and
I *guarantee* you the rest of The Wing won't be happy with
Ronnie, either. And Braxton is a small place. Funny things
happen with steel around there."

"I get it," she said.

"Do you?" Jadick asked.

"Yeah, Emil. It's simple and I understand you all's sort
of subtraction."

This Dean Pugh character would need close watching.
He was foul and lean, junk-food raised and opposed to
dentistry judging by his greening teeth. His skin had a
yellow tinge, beneath shit-fly green eyes, and his brain was
possibly odd enough to posthumously set off a bidding
frenzy among scientists. He generally seemed batty as a
loon, goofy as a goose on ice, immaculately weird, with
no stain of normalcy on him at all.

And Cecil Byrne was his *friend*.

They could have Ronnie killed with a phone call.

"I'll get right on checkin' out the next place," she said,
looking down. "It might take awhile to find."

"That's what The Wing wants to hear," Jadick said pleasantly. "Us and Ronnie and you, we're going to use this town to get even."

"Even with what?"

"Just even," he said. "That's what everybody really wants, is to get even."

"If gettin' even is so hot," Wanda said, absently rubbing a flat palm over her midriff while staring out through the porch door, "how come nobody ever stops there?"

In the wee hours she said, "I'd like it if you'd shut the bedroom door first."

"Ain't we delicate?" Jadick said, but he did close the door. A thick red candle sat before a vanity mirror, filling the room with soft, waltzing light. Emil pulled his shirt off, looking down at Wanda, who lay on her back on the bed, watching him. He checked himself out in the mirror, admiring the jailhouse sculpture he'd pumped his body into being. "I'm as strong as I look, too," he said.

"I know," she said. Last week Wanda had thrown him a fuck to seal the pact, and, though she'd done it out of a sense of duty, she'd been shocked at how badly she desired this duty. She had nimble fingers, a dirty mind, and plenty of privacy in which she'd utilized the two, but it had been a long time between injections of the real. "Your tummy is the strongest one I've ever seen in person."

Jadick smiled.

"Three hundred sit-ups a day, pun-kin. Nothin' else to do in Braxton, you know. Locked up like that, you get into fitness." Jadick had short, limp black hair, a stumpy neck, and muscles everywhere. His face was wide and flat, a common enough look back in Parma, Ohio, a bohunk, polack, et cetera section of Cleveland. "With baby oil," he said, "my body's a real slick temple."

Suddenly his face split with a wide smile.

"I got something for you," he said. "Answer me this— what's the most romantic word there is?"

Wanda stared at him dully, showing him that tough expression she generally showed the world.

"Ouch?" she said.

"Ouch?" He looked at her with his eyes narrowed. "No, no, ouch is the *second* most romantic, there, punkin." He reached into his pants pocket and brought out a handful of rings. "Diamonds, Wanda. *Diamond* is the number one most romantic word."

The bed was a Salvation Army bargain, a mottled pink mattress tossed on the wooden floor. Jadick sat on the edge and lifted Wanda's left hand. He held various rings up to her fingers, then pushed a nice showy one on, shoving it up next to her wedding band.

"Wanda," he said in a childish, playful tone, "will you be my valentine?"

"Valentine's is long past, Emil."

"Yeah, that's right," he said. He slid his hands between her shiny white shorts and her ass, palms up, and squeezed. "So, you wanna fuck?"

She smiled up at him and his highly defined arms and chest, and said, "I'm too worn out to scream."

Jadick pulled his hands free, then stood. He positioned himself so that he was visible in the mirror. As he undid his trousers he fixed his face into a stern but smoldering expression. He kicked his slacks off, then stood on the bed over Wanda, and put his hands on his hips and flexed here, there, and all over. She went, "Mmm," and he slowly lowered himself until he was kneeling between her legs. His hands went back to her hard round ass and as he lifted her up, he pulled the shorts apart at the seams, then raised her higher, his eyes on hers, and higher still, then licked her buttocks and ran his tongue straight up through the wetness to her belly button. He sprang forward on his knees, beneath her, and lowered her onto his cock, pushed her back flat and thrust hard once, then raised himself on stiffened arms. A bead of sweat ran down his nose as he glared at her from above, and he gruffly said, "Ouch, huh?"

The dawn came on, pink and sweet, to find Emil Jadick sitting bare-assed on the back porch, having an eye-opener of beer. Somehow, being down here in chitlin country made him feel reflective. He was now at that jarring, mid-thirties turning point, that age where persistent losers often decide that the cause of their failure is not lack of talent, but scope. Yeah. That's it. Something big, something truly audacious, would cause that self-rumored talent to boil to the top and be seen.

Taking over all the night action and daylight graft of an entire redneck town—that was something big. And The Wing was the crew to do it, too. With himself in charge, why, only bad luck could mess it up.

The Wing was a white prison gang, a loose nationwide cartel of sorts that kept in touch via three-to-five jolts and visitation privileges. Though not as strong as The Aryan Brotherhood or The Brown Mafia or The Locked-Up Muslims, The Wing had dirty fingers that could pull triggers on both sides of those high federal walls. Federal prisons served as a kind of criminal headhunter's service bringing hoods and hustlers from all parts of the nation into contact, and this led to frequent yardbird seminars on how we did this in Chicago, L.A., Boston, or Louisiana, and how it will work *even better* next time now that this rap has highlighted the flaws in the gambit.

As the bayou sounds shrank from the growing light, Jadick felt strong. Dean and Cecil were in the front room, snoring in each other's arms, but ready to back any play he made. The Wing planned for him to raise the financing with Wanda's help, then in a short while, Ronnie and a dozen others would be paroled, sprung from joints across the country. They'd roll right over this Auguste Beaurain asshole. No question about it. Things would be changed then. Some members of The Wing held odd religious opinions that not only did not rule out a life of crime, but, in fact, made it seem a holy path to trod in the service of a truly deciphered Lord. None of that shit mattered to Jadick for he merely wanted to be with a strong set of movers, and if what he was up to was in any way religious, he knew that he was only on the muscle end of that theology, looking for a way to shake down the future.

"Mornin'," Wanda said. She came onto the porch carrying the rags her shiny shorts had become. She took a seat next to Jadick. "I'll make biscuits and gravy."

"Fine."

"Oh, man," she said, "I'm drippin'." She began to swab at her crotch with the shorts, her head down. "Emil, I wonder what my husband thinks about all I'm doin' for him."

"Pun-kin," Jadick said, staring out across the backwater mire. "I don't see how Ronnie could be anything but proud of you."

4

From the winging city pigeon's vantage point the neighborhoods of St. Bruno looked like a fist clutching at the lifeline that was the big greasy river. There, to the south, perched on a few modest mounds, was Hawthorne Hills, a reserve for the tony, where neocolonial was the favored architecture and attitude. The next thing upriver was the south side, a downtrodden but proud throng of streets, where the architecture had been inspired by the simple square, to no one's aesthetic pleasure. There was a vast midtown to be seen from an avian perspective; the seat of government was there by day, in the center of a warehouse district, and by night it was the preferred falling-down spot for winos and otherwise addled seekers. Up the hill from the river was Frechette Park, a surprisingly well-kept sprawl of greenery, and next to it Pan Fry, the longtime black neighborhood where the housing was HUD approved and roundballs of various sizes and snowcapped schemes offered the dreamy ways to better quarters. On down the hill, sprung up from the wet land, there was Frogtown, the white-trash Paris, where the wide brown flow of rank water scented all the days, and every set of toes touched bottom.

And down below, in the formative stage of the day, on a Frogtown street of frail frame houses, Detective How Blanchette stood on the porch of one rented to Miss N. Webb, and pounded against the door.

Presently the thick, inner door cracked open and Rene Shade bent around it, just his head showing behind the screen.

"How."

"Sorry, Rene. We got business."

"Come on in."

Shade backed into the living room, a space dominated by several travel posters of America with Italian writing on them, and a huge Persian rug with a path worn diagonally across the rich intricacies. Shade wore only a black T-shirt and he collapsed groggily onto a couch and bent over to strap on his ankle holster.

"I still feel hammered," he said. "I don't know where my pants are."

Blanchette held out a pair of khaki trousers, then threw them at his partner.

"I found 'em on the porch, you pervert."

"Oh, yeah," Shade said, red-eyed and smiling. "Now I remember." He stood and stepped into the pants, then, just as he latched the buckle he said, "Hey, my vacation starts in about an hour, How."

"'Fraid not."

"'Fraid *so*," Shade said. "We're off to the Ouachitas to feed fish to the eagles, sleep in the mud."

How Blanchette was sandy-haired and ruggedly chubby, with an innocent moon face and a cynical manner. Porkpie hats had never gone out of style with him and he was now, as usual, in his black leather trench coat which he believed trimmed twenty pounds from his shadow. His shirt and slacks were part of a large acquisition he'd made of fire-sale plaids, and he smoked a ten-cent panatela.

"The Captain canceled it," he said. "We've got some serious business at hand."

"It can't be serious enough to keep me here when the trout are biting."

"Rene, a cop got whacked. Shot four times, he was, then dumped in front of St. Joe's emergency room."

"Who?"

"A Patrolman Gerald Bell—know him?"

"Not really. Maybe if I saw him."

"Well, I just did and he don't look like anybody anymore."

Shade rubbed his fingers on his cheeks, then pulled his hands up and straight across his hair.

"I don't want to wake her," he said. "I'll leave a note."

"Do it quick," Blanchette said, then raised his nose and elaborately sniffed the air three times. "And get in there and wash your face, too. You smell like yesterday's fish."

Blanchette drove the city-issue Chevy and Shade followed him in his own blue Nova. They went crosstown to the south side where Gerald Bell had shared a home with his father.

The small square white house was at the very dead end of Nott Street, perched just above a wide ravine. Old refrigerators, rusty tin cans, and assorted trash of varying vintages littered the ravine, making it an attractive playground to boys and disease.

Shade and Blanchette went up the gray slab steps to the side door which they knew from long experience would open directly to the kitchen. The inner door was swung back and through the screen they heard music and smelled a wonderful, simmering aroma.

Before they could knock a voice from inside said, "Uh-oh, who the hell are you guys?"

"Police, Mr. Bell," Shade said, "can we come in?"

"Gerry's not here, fellas," Ray Bell said. He walked over and stood close to the screen. He was a short old sport, with thin white hair, a messed-up nose that undoubtedly had an interesting story behind it, and a retiree's pleasant paunch. "He must have scored some poon last night. I been waiting for him to drag on in."

"That's why we're here," Blanchette said.

Bell's lower lip drooped.

"Oh," he said, and let them in. They showed him their shields and he nodded absently, then took a seat at the small kitchen table. He slapped a radio and killed the country music. A heavy black kettle steamed on the stove, and the bubbling red sauce in it filled the air with a savory scent. "Is he dead?"

"Yes, sir," Shade said.

Blanchette went over toward the sweet sauce and stood near it, then lowered his head and inhaled, his eyebrows raising with approval.

"You know," Bell said as he watched the kettle, "that sauce, why, it seems like an omen. Bad luck, I guess. You know, Ramona, the wife, she died a year ago, right about where you're standin'. Too many years of bacon I guess. That's what they say anyhow. All that grease. We was raised on the stuff, or worse. You know what was cookin'?

31

Right, that sauce. I was cookin' up some of that sauce 'cause I wanted a ham basted slow and she come in here and said, 'Can I help?' and keeled over practically dead before I could even answer. It makes me feel like I'm to blame for not pickin' up the signs from God, 'cause today is the first time I made up a batch since then." He lowered his head and growled sadly, like a wounded thing. "Oh, fellas, there's a bottle of Rebel Yell in that cabinet, there. Be good to me."

Shade fetched the bottle and set it in front of Bell.

Bell unscrewed the lid and took a tentative sip of the bourbon, then raised it again and chugged. After lowering the bottle he wiped his mouth with the back of his hand.

"What happened to my boy?"

"Shot to death," Blanchette said. He was taste-testing the red sauce, slurping off the ladle. "Don't know where he was killed but his body was dropped off at St. Joe's. He'd been dead a couple of hours already."

"Christ almighty," Bell said. "Man, I've got to wonder who'd have the stones to do that on a cop. Don't you all wonder that?"

"He was in civvies."

"Well, sure." Bell took another drink. "He was off duty."

Shade sat at the table across from Bell. Last night's cocktail fog was slowly evaporating and he was finally beginning to feel awake.

"I didn't know your boy," he said, "but we can't have this, Mr. Bell. Nobody wants to stand for cops getting whacked out like street slime."

"I know that," Bell said. "I was raised up here, in this town, and I always have noticed this strange thing that

32

when a St. Bruno cop gets powdered, pretty soon after that one or two or even three street studs turn up, shot dead tryin' to escape. I know the drill, Detective, and don't change it now."

Blanchette, the dripping ladle in his hand, said, "Did your kid tramp his dick across private property, stuff like that? I mean, whoever took him off made him wince a good bit first." He licked the spoon, then ran his tongue over his lips. "Could've been a pissed-off husband type."

"I resent that," Bell said. His eyes had a sad, shiny look to them. He shoved up from his chair and took the ladle away from Blanchette. "I resent that comment about my dead son 'cause he wouldn't screw no married woman. Not unless he won the tail in a Hold 'Em game, at least." He put the big spoon into the kettle and began to stir. "If it was anything that got him in a jam that's what it'd be— the gamblin'."

"Was he a big gambler?" Shade asked.

"Naw, but he kept tryin' to be." Bell reached above the stove to the spice rack and selected a bottle of ground cayenne and shook it over the sauce. "If he won today he lost tomorrow. He was searchin' for consistency but it eluded him. I would reckon he was the sort of gambler all the *real* gamblers are always glad to see at the table."

"So he was a regular loser, uh?"

"He didn't call it that." Bell was now grabbing spice tins at random, and dumping what would certainly be an original and zesty blend into the sauce. The big spoon scraped against the kettle gratingly. "No, he didn't call himself a regular loser. He said he was a fella with a system." The old man looked older, and weak and weepy. "Oh, you boys have took my legs out from under me." He turned and leaned against the counter, the ladle held at midthigh, dripping long red streaks down his legs. "I'm goin' to tell you all some stuff you'll know pretty soon anyway. Gerry, I think he owed money or something. I heard he stood shotgun at crap games and such. This is what I heard but he wouldn't answer me when I brought it up. He only said, 'We both like to eat, Pop.'" Bell noted the streaks sliding down his legs and set the ladle on the stove. "You fellas, you're local, you know how it is. It's the same as always. Most everybody around here'll bet on which is the dry side of a raindrop or what hydrant a dog'll piss on. Gamblin' has always been more or less open here."

"Look," Shade said, "we won't do anything to make your boy look bad." Shade pulled the Rebel Yell near and sniffed the whiskey, then screwed the cap back on. "What aren't you telling us, Mr. Bell?"

"Aw, I heard something else. I was at Johnny's Shamrock awhile back and some of the talk there was about Gerry."

Blanchette lifted the ladle, smelled the blindly spiced sauce, and poured it back.

"Spit it out, sport," he said. "What were they gabbin' about at The Shamrock?"

"Now you, you're a rude motherfucker, ain't you?" Bell said. He pointed a gnarled finger in Blanchette's face.

"My mother's dead," Blanchette said, smiling slightly as he generally did when called a name. "The rest of it is personality."

"I see," Bell said. "A defective." He dropped his hand back to his side. "What I heard at The Shamrock was that Gerry, Gerry, maybe, possibly, had took a little battin' practice on some Frogtowner's kneecap." Bell raised his

34

hands and spread them. "He's gone now, ain't he? But that's what they were sayin'."

Shade stood up from the table and passed the whiskey to the trembling, sagging man.

"They say who it was?" he asked.

"Um-hmm." Bell gulped a slug of sour mash, and sniffled. "Willie Dastillon—know him?"

"Like a dog knows fleas," Shade said. "We'll check it out. You got any relatives who can sit with you today?"

"You better believe it," Bell said. "You cops better straighten this out before we do. I was pretty tough once."

"Naw, shit," Shade said, "none of that. Have a wake, or whatever, belt out some prayers, but don't get in our way. Your boy was one of ours, mister. We'll take care of it."

"Go do it then." Bell faced the stove and the boiling sauce and shuddered, then lifted the hot kettle bare-handed and slopped the whole bucket into the sink, splattering the walls and counter top. He put his quickly blistering hands beneath cold tap water and said, "I ain't eatin' today."

Grif's Grubbery was a breakfast and lunch place set under a warehouse at the city market, in midtown. There was no sign out front, but forty years of word-of-mouth had caused the steps leading down from the street to become worn and smooth. It was a cozy, triangular room, with a short counter at the apex and long, communal tables in the open area.

Shade and Blanchette sat at the counter in the poorly lighted room. Grif Rosten, the owner, leaned his lanky, knobby self over the counter at the other end where he was using his side of a three-way conversation to lecture two young teamsters on the Haymarket Riot, the Reuther brothers, and other topics they deemed musty and evinced no interest in. Grif had boxcarred into town in the thirties from the West Coast where he claimed to have known Harry Bridges, Max Baer, and oriental ways of love. Though his historical and cultural hectoring resulted in frequent offers of bus tickets back to Oakland, the food kept the diner packed.

"Well," Blanchette said, "I think it might turn out that Officer Bell was a scandal waitin' to happen. That's what it looks like to me. Hey, Grif! Grif, we're hungry down here!"

"It wasn't Willie Dastillon," Shade said as Rosten slowly came toward them. "Willie might steal a hen but he wouldn't break an egg."

Rosten had slightly more than a basic issue of nose and long thin white hair that curled up at the back of his neck. He stood behind the counter, wiping his hands on a big red bib he always wore that had Texas Chili Burn-Off stitched in a circle on the front.

"Oh," he said, "the fat guy and the pug're hungry. So they yell at me. That was a yell, wasn't it? It sounded like a shout to me. A yell, a shout."

Shade was merely a customer to Rosten, but he knew that Blanchette and Grif were, behind a façade of insults, friends. It was one of those odd couplings of disparate personalities, and he understood that they frequently went duck hunting together, split a bottle of Glenlivet, or drove to Beale Street and acted shameless.

"Rosten, we're in a hurry," Blanchette said. "I'll have the usual. Rene?"

"Tomato juice," Shade said. His tongue was furry, his

mouth tasted like barroom floor grunge, and his eyes felt dry. "And some of those buttermilk biscuits with gravy."

Rosten wrote the order on a small pad.

"Hung over are you, Shade?"

"I guess."

"Uh-huh," Rosten said and raised his brows. "You ever think maybe you're brain-damaged a little bit, there, Shade? Ever wonder if maybe old Foster Broome didn't jab-and-hook some useful knowledge right out of your brain?"

"I know he did," Shade said, looking up with a red baleful gaze. "But what it was that he beat out of me was all those general rules about how young guys ain't s'posed to pound on old white-haired wiseasses just to hear 'em go 'squish.' I have to work real hard to remember that one, Grif. I'm real hazy on it. Squish is a beautiful sound. Bring me some eats, huh?"

"Hey," Rosten said as he moved toward the kitchen, "just fillin' you in on the AMA report, champ."

When Rosten was gone and the knife-and-fork hubbub of the room had made silence tiresome, Blanchette said, "Lighten up, Rene. After we eat go home, clean up, and so forth. This thing is goin' to be a full-tilt fuckin' boogie 'til we find the perp, dig?"

"Yeah," Shade answered. "He's all right. I know he's your buddy."

"Forget that," Blanchette said. He was sucking away at a soggy cigar, his coat and hat still on. "After you get cleaned up you go see Willie. I'll head back to Second Street. Bell's partner, a guy named Thomas Mouton, is supposed to be there. You see your old pal Willie, then meet me and Mouton at the station."

"Right," Shade answered. "If I can stay awake."

"You want a black beauty, there, sleepyhead?"

"Naw," Shade said. "I don't like the way I talk behind that shit."

"Good," Blanchette said. "I don't know if I have any anyhow. Knock back some of Rosten's joe."

Shade walked over to the coffeepots and helped himself to a cup. He then returned to his stool and blew on the joe.

When Rosten brought on the chow Shade was, as always, taken slightly aback at Blanchette's "usual" breakfast. He had two pork chops seasoned with fennel and skillet-fried, thick white gravy over biscuits, three eggs beat to a sludge and cooked soft, and a butterscotch shake. It was the idea of shakes before noon that put Shade over the edge.

"You are a marvel," he said to Blanchette whose mouth was otherwise employed, prompting a grunt in response. "Most guys who eat like you would get fat or something."

"Uhnn," Blanchette responded, nodding as he wrapped up a chew. He picked up a pork chop and tore the perimeter of fat away, stacking the greasy, undesirable, slivers on the side of his plate. "That's my secret," he said; then, with one big sucking chomp, he turned the chop into a bone.

"You mean not chewing?" Shade asked. "That's your secret?"

"And trimmin' the fat," Blanchette answered. "Plus, let's face it— I am a little bit stout."

"Really? I guess I never noticed." Shade was shoving the biscuits around on his own plate, familiarizing himself with his breakfast before eating it. "I mean, those fuckin' plaids you're always wearing, How, they make bein' super-chunky seem sort of secondary."

"Uh-oh! You're on to *all* my secrets now."

Over the next few minutes Shade managed to eat a biscuit or two and Blanchette cleaned his own plate. They sipped coffee and Blanchette probed his teeth with a mint toothpick.

Rosten came down the counter and stood near them.

"What's new, How?"

"Well, actually," Blanchette said, "I'm glad you asked that. I want the two of you both to hear this at once. I don't play favorites." Blanchette rested the toothpick in the corner of his mouth, pulled his hat off and fanned his face with it. "Look, fellas, last night, it was a good night. The weather was decent, the Cardinals won, and I was hungry."

"Imagine that," Rosten said.

"Hush up," Blanchette said. "This is hard enough, man." He put his hat back on. "I was *hungry* so I went to Paquet's and had me some shrimp boiled in beer, and some of that yellow rice and a gallon or two of some kind of wine they had that I found out I could stand to drink, and right after stiffin' the waiter for bein' such a snot, I leaned over and asked Molly Paddock to marry me."

Rosten responded by shaking his head as if there were a terrible buzzing in his ears.

Shade said, "Man, what brought this on?"

"Well," Blanchette said, "I'll tell you what it was. What it was, is I been seein' Molly for three years and, let's face it, the young succulents were pretty good at brushin' me off and she doesn't. That attracts you to a person, when they don't brush you off and you're a guy like me. So, young succulents ain't gonna wet down my future, and I know it, and the other day I patted my middle. I patted my middle and my hand clinched around the fringe of a great gob of flab. It was then I said to myself— 'How, you're so fat, you might as well go ahead and get married.'"

"That's a dandy reason to throw in the towel," Shade said. He thought of Molly Paddock, a decent, bland-faced shapeless cop-widow with a pleasant personality and no ambition at all. "I guess congrats are in order."

"Most people would think so," Blanchette said. "And what do you think about me gettin' married, Grif?"

Rosten put two long fingers to his chin and cocked his head sideways.

"I think it's a crime against women," he said.

"You shit head."

"I don't think you'll be indicted on it."

"You know-it-all shit head," Blanchette said as he stood. He tossed a bill onto the counter. He looked at Rosten. "You just couldn't say something nice, could you?"

"I want to," Rosten said, "but I'm cursed with honesty."

Shade tossed down a buck and a half and he and Blanchette shuffled out of The Grubbery and up the worn steps to the street. The whole workaday world was out and about, honking horns, grinding gears on produce trucks, walking along with eyes down.

When they reached the parking lot Shade said, "You got any ups, How?"

"I thought you didn't want any."

"I don't but I might need it. I'm pooped, man. I was drinkin' 'til four or five in the morning."

40

Blanchette pulled out his wallet and slid an Alka-Seltzer foil from a credit-card slot. He handed it to Shade. "I only got this one," he said. "It'll put some zest in your fuckin' day, too."

As he walked to his own car Shade said, "I just want it in case I need it."

"Naturally, comrade," Blanchette said. "But I'll bet you do."

5

After breakfast Shade decided to cut the sensitive noses of the world some slack, and went home to take a shower. His apartment was a small historical curio, with furniture from the fifties, plumbing from the forties, on the second floor of a brick row house that had been built by French craftsmen who'd all been dead for a minimum of one hundred and twenty years.

Shade's mother lived downstairs and ran a poolroom from what had once been the dining and living rooms. Though still married to the ever-drifting John X. Shade, she had reverted to her maiden name for business, and called the modest establishment Ma Blanqui's Pool House.

When Shade stepped out of the shower feeling Irish Springy, he dried and dressed in light cotton. The heat would rise through the day so he selected white pants, loose and pleated, a yellow pullover that billowed out enough to hide the pistol clipped at his belt, and went sockless in his stinky white slip-ons that he felt he could run faster in.

Shade had lived in this same building for most of his life, here at the corner of Lafitte and Perry, and learned the hard lessons of the world on these hard bricked streets, within spitting distance of home. This was Frogtown, where the sideburns were longer, the fuses shorter, the skirts higher, and the expectations lower, and he loved it.

As he came down the back stairs he could see the river across the tracks, and a shimmery haze rose from it, making the farther shore a mere mirage. He slid into his car, fired the husky-sounding three twenty-seven, and headed toward the nearby abode of Willie Dastillon.

Willie Dastillon, like most good Americans, wanted to "have it all," and to him that meant having a door jimmy, a friendly fence, and a ten-minute headstart. He lived in a small frame house with green tar-paper siding on Voltaire Street.

When Shade came up the steps to the porch a small, bruised boy was wheeling a tricycle recklessly from rail to rail.

"Who you?" he asked as Shade approached.

"I'm looking for your dad. Is Willie home?"

"Mm-hmm." The boy jumped off the tricycle and reached above his head to the front doorknob. He opened the door with surprising ease. "Papa! Papa, a mister is here."

Shade stepped inside without being invited. Willie sat in the front room. His left leg was in a cast and propped up on a stool. He wore sunglasses and earphones, and held a long white back scratcher that he plucked at air-guitar style.

When he saw Shade he pulled the earphones down to his neck and Jason and the Scorchers rattled against his throat. He then shook his head and killed the music.

"Shut the door, Mick. Go back out and play."

"Okay, Papa."

Shade helped himself to a seat.

"Right, make yourself at home," Willie said. "Today must be the day of the party. I guess I forgot."

Willie Dastillon was rock-and-roll lean with a long shag of dark hair and from his left ear dangled a glittering shank of earring that might have pulled in a keeper bass if it were trolled near rocks. His nose was narrow with a sharp, balloon-busting tip, and his cheeks were blue with stubble. He wore a black .38 Special T-shirt and a pair of blue work pants with the left leg hacked off above the cast.

"Did you just drop by to watch me jam on my back scratcher, Shade?"

Shade leaned back in the soft chair and put his feet on the coffee table. His expression was flat and he stared unblinkingly at Willie.

"Is your whole band going to wear casts, Willie? I mean, I'm not up to the minute on rock theatrics, but a whole band in casts, why, that'd be a gimmick, but maybe not a good one."

"Hey," Willie said, "there's a thought. I'll bring it up with the guys. I wouldn't mind puttin' the drummer in a full body cast, man. He shows up on time but he just can't *keep* time."

Willie Dastillon was a thief and a gambler but he called himself a musician. He'd had several local bands over the years but B&E busts and the pursuit of bliss in powder form had kept any from lasting more than a summer. The bruised child and wife who worked while he didn't were both testaments to his callous vanity, for the man blew enough on craps alone for them to live much better. He'd bet Betty's next paycheck on a fighter he'd never seen before, or those splayfooted ponies, or them rolling bones. He was a man with a tin-ear present who dreamed of a rock-opera future.

"What happened to your leg?" Shade asked.

"The usual: I was backstage at a Stones concert out there in L.A. and, you see, my buddy, ol' Jack Nicholson who is just a card and a half, says to me, 'Willie, go on out there and turn your pipes loose on "Beast of Burden," and shame Jagger off the fuckin' stage.' So, because me and Jack are like this, I go out there and Keith Richards nods and smiles and Jagger bows at me and hands me the mike, and all these flowers are tossed onstage and flashbulbs are poppin' and all I can see is a wave of young titties bouncin' in front of me, and I get confused and fall off the fuckin' runway, break the leg. You can hear the pop on their live album, man."

"Yeah, right," Shade said. "I think I was there, too, singing harmony, wasn't I? Next time you tell it, could you mention I was there, too, Willie?"

"Depends on who I'm tellin' it to, Shade. In some circles your name ain't a charm."

Shade took note of the way the earring Willie wore flipped up and down with his every head movement, and asked, "What is it with earrings, anyway?"

"Hunh?" Willie's fingers were touched to the shimmery ornament. "It's fashion."

"That's all—just fashion?"

"Uh-huh. All my crowd has 'em."

"It doesn't mean anything? It doesn't mean, 'Hey, I'm for social justice,' or 'Party 'til you puke,' or 'Meet me in the men's room,' or nothing?"

"No, man. No. It's all about fashion." Willie turned his head to the side so Shade had a close-up view of the earring. "I just got this one, man, whatta you think?"

Shade pursed his lips and nodded slowly.

"It's very fashionable, Willie." Shade leaned over and tapped the cast on Willie's leg. "I got some questions for you."

"I knew you would." Willie pushed on the bridge of his sunglasses as if he were adding camouflage to a hiding spot. "I ain't the answer man, though."

"There is a rumor making the rounds that a cop did some leg busting around here, either as a public service or a second job, I don't know which. But the rumor is he did some unlicensed chiropracty hereabouts with a fungo."

"Cops are here to protect us," Willie said, smirking beneath his Ray-Bans, "not to hurt us."

"Look, Willie," Shade said, "I want to know if a cop named Bell broke your fucking leg, so what I'm going to do is, I'm going to ask you, 'Did a cop named Bell break your fucking leg?' and that'll give you the opportunity to answer yes or no and if you do that and I believe you I won't have to go gorilla on you."

"I heard that's your specialty, Shade." Willie slid his hands up and down the back scratcher like he was strumming chords, and looked to the ceiling, lost in a silent solo.

"That's right," Shade said. He leaned over and shoved the cast off the stool. Then he stood and slapped the sunglasses from Willie's face. "I *have* been accused of being a brute before, son. Several times. I think you should know I lived with the shame of it all just fine."

Willie rubbed two fingers at the bridge of his nose, a gesture of impatience and disdain.

"You really think I'm goin' to do a bad-mouth testimony on one cop to another? Shit, man, you seem to have your mind made up anyhow. Here I am, crippled up 'til practically Halloween, and you're jerkin' me 'round 'cause I *might* be a victim." He retrieved his sunglasses from the floor beside him and slid back under them. "What gets you interested anyhow? He cut you out of your piece of the ice, man?"

Shade, who considered himself to be prey to many of the nasty passions, felt that while he could be brutish or dense, slow or too quick, he could not be bought by any valuable thing that had numbers on it. This quality seemed so mulish for a human to possess that he found perverse pride in the fact that his corruptibility took a form closer to the poetic than the crass.

So he slapped those cheesy shades from the man's face again.

Willie's face firmed into a somewhat impotent expression of anger.

"You fucker," he said and started to rise, crippled or not. "This is my house."

"Freeze on that," Shade said softly. "You ain't got the whiskers and we both know it." Shade shook his head and picked up the glasses and handed them back to Willie. "I'm tired, son, that's all. Forgive me." He sat on the arm of Willie's chair and patted him on the head. "Could you find it in your little nubbin of a heart to forgive me?" For the first time now the heavy metal thief seemed scared. "See, Officer Bell was whacked last night, there, superstar, and under the first rock we turned over we found *your* name."

"Oh, shit, man, you can't think . . ."

"You see the spot you're in now, don't you?"

47

The sudden recognition of the spot he was in set Willie squirming, tapping the plastic fingered back scratcher against his cast.

"You know I couldn't do that," he said. "Let's face it, man, I know what I am. I'm a musician who never caught a break so I *find* tape decks in other people's cars and shit like that. I dig gamblin', too, and natch I love my tunes, but stealin's only just my way to platinum—you know I'd never shoot anybody, especially Gerry Bell."

"Gerry, huh?" Shade said. "So you know him?"

"Hey, lots of us small fry got to know Officer Bell, man." Willie put his hand over his mouth and squeezed his lips, then said, "Since he's dead I'll tell you, Shade. Yeah, fuckin' Bell broke my leg all right, right here in this room, in front of Betty, too. He come in here in his fuckin' *uniform* to collect from me and I was tapped for cash so he tosses a quarter at my face and says, 'That's for my ticket, punk, I always pay for a good time.' Then he did it, man. Hurt like a motherfucker."

"Did his partner, Mouton, come with him?"

"He sat out in the patrol car."

As Shade pondered the implications of Bell's brand of civic duty, the front door opened and in came little Mick.

"Can we eat?" he asked. There were scabs on his elbows, bruises on his legs and dirt in his ears. "Papa, I'm hungry."

"So eat," Willie said. "Get yourself a hot dog."

"Mom said I'm not s'posed to touch the stove."

"Then *don't* touch it, boy. Eat 'em cold. They're good that way. Wrap a piece of bread around one and eat it cold."

Mick padded off toward the kitchen, his head down,

the slump of his shoulders giving an advance notice of his opinion on eating hot dogs cold.

"Willie," Shade said, "aren't you going to get up off your ass, stump in there and feed the kid?"

"This cast feels like a ball an' chain, man. Makes my hip hurt to walk on it."

Shade, who found that all bad fathers reminded him of his own, said, "Dastillon, shit floats and you're rising fast."

"He can fend for his ownself," Willie said defensively. "I always had to. Nobody fed me but my own sticky fingers."

"I'll go cook the kid a couple of dogs," Shade said and started toward the kitchen.

"You do that, Shade, but don't spoil him. The world ain't no day-care center and I'm teachin' him that now, while he's young, so he won't be all let down when he grows up."

There it was, Shade thought, the Frogtown ethic in one bumper-slogan line, The World Ain't No Day-care Center.

The kitchen was orderly and clean, a testimony to Betty's elbow exercise. Shade found a black skillet in the oven and set it on a burner. He opened the fridge and saw half a dozen short dogs of wine and back behind a container of yogurt he turned up a pack of red dogs of chicken.

"How many you want, tiger?" he asked Mick.

"This many," Mick said, holding up two fingers.

Shade turned on the gas beneath the skillet and dropped the dogs in. He found a fork in a drawer and used it to shove the links around.

"Hey!" Willie shouted from the front room. "Hey, put me on about three, too, uh? I'm laid up."

"I can't hear you," Shade barked back.

While the chill was grilled from the dogs Mick got out two slices of bread and squeezed mustard onto them. Shade had the heat on high and the dogs were soon sizzling. He turned the flame off and handed the fork to the boy.

"Bon appetit, tiger."

Shade went back to the living room and stood over Willie.

"Okay, Willie, the domestic shit ain't free. Who was Bell collecting for?"

"Come on, man, you're from around here—take a guess."

"Rudy Regot? Delbert McKechnie? Shuggie Zeck?"

"Yeah, Shuggie," Willie said. "Am I fuckin' up major tellin' you this? I mean, I heard you and him was runnin' mates back there in yesteryear."

"You heard that, huh?"

"Everybody has. I'll bet you were a troublesome pair of playmates."

"You're right, Willie, that's all back there in yesteryear." Shade once again sat beside Willie. "So what's his beef with you?"

"You know me, man. I thought I had me a new seven-card system, but, really, I guess what I got is a disease. That's what Betty says ten or fifty times a day. Nothin' out of the ordinary, I was tryin' to work the kinks out of the system and dropped a bunch of dinero I didn't actually have. Officer Bell encouraged me to come up with it."

"Did you?"

"You fuckin' A, I did. Sold the car, I only got two legs.

Now Betty hoofs it to work. Lucky her, I'm crippled up 'til the wet season ends." He edged the scratcher under his cast and pulled it up and down. "The man took some pleasure in it, too. You'd've thought he was porkin' Tina Turner, 'stead of crushin' *my* bones, from the look on his face."

"You know for sure Shuggie sent him?"

"Well, it was Shuggie's game where I got the markers, but Shuggie is gettin' up there, Shade. He's like this with Mr. B. now I hear."

"Everybody's heard that."

"Gee, sorry to be a borin' snitch, man." Willie rocked back and plucked away at the back scratcher. "You find who killed this bad cop Bell tell 'em I'll play a benefit for their defense fund, huh?"

Mick had come to stand in the doorway of the kitchen, a hot dog in each hand.

"Did Bell work for Shuggie?"

"I don't fuckin' know, man. I don't really know the big answers but what I do know—duh-dun-duh-dun—is the blues. What else can I say?"

"Nothing good," Shade said. He walked to the door and opened it, and as he stepped out into the hot wet air of another tough day in river country, he heard Willie bark, "Come 'ere, give me one of those!"

6

The police station was on Second Street, a white-stone building erected along severely square lines, at hand-holding distance from city hall.

When Shade came up the stone steps, steps polished to a fine sheen by the somber gait of the guilty, the light dancing feet of the innocent, and the uncertain shuffle of the uncertain, he turned right toward the squad room just as How Blanchette came down the adjoining hallway from the Captain's office.

"What's up, How?" Shade asked. "Bell's partner here?"

"Yeah," Blanchette said, "he's downstairs." He held his hat in his hand and there was a pinkish flush to his face. "We been split up, Rene. Captain took me away from you and put me with Jesse Pickett."

"What?" Shade asked. "Am I in trouble?"

"I don't think so yet," Blanchette said as he shook his head and wiped sweat from his cheeks. "Officially, me and Pickett are supposed to say we're in charge of the investigation. Pickett's okay, I can live with Pickett, but I don't know why they broke us up."

"They?"

"Mayor Crawford's in there, too, baby. He's got a new look. When you go in there you'll notice it."

"I'm supposed to go in there, huh? When?"

"Now, comrade," Blanchette said. "And I think you better have an open mind."

The heavy wooden door to Captain Karl Bauer's office was open, so Shade looked in and said, "You wanted to see me?"

"That's right, Shade. Come in here and close that thing behind you." Bauer pointed at a chair directly in front of his desk. "Give your dogs a rest, Detective, we have a thing or two to discuss."

Shade sat in the chair, a bit tentatively since a vast range of unpleasant possible topics for discussion wisped through his mind like paranoid vapors.

"What's the deal, Captain? I already talked to Blanchette."

"Uh-huh. Good." Bauer was a large, flat-topped man, with pale skin that had been acned and pitted so that it resembled a cob cleaned of corn, eyes the color of snuff, and the general expression of a natural-born straw boss. "Officer Bell's murder is going to require a kind of unique approach, Shade, and you've been picked to make it."

From the far corner of his left eye Shade became aware of another presence in the room. He turned that way, and back there in a shadowy part of the office, seated on a straight-backed chair, he saw a gargoyle in silk watching him closely. Mayor Gene Crawford's silver hair was, as usual, combed just so, and his suit had that sheer and costly look, but his face was interestingly made over. His eyes were swollen nearly closed, with black half-moons below the slits, and a piece of aluminum had been taped over an obviously smashed nose.

"Look at me, Shade," Bauer said. "I'm the one talking to you."

Shade faced him across the polished mahogany.

"Yes, sir."

"Did you hear what I said? I said we're going to try a unique approach using you. How's that sound?"

"I'm listening, Captain."

"Fine. What do you know about Officer Bell?"

"I heard he moonlighted as a collector for a loan shark, and that he did the collecting in uniform with a non-regulation fungo bat."

"That's what you heard, huh?" Bauer leaned back in his chair, then rocked squeakingly back and forth. "Anything else?"

"Not yet."

"I see." Bauer leaned forward suddenly and put his elbows on his desk, making dramatic eye contact with Shade. "Here and now I'm going to tell you how Bell got his dumb-ass self greased, Shade. I'm telling you 'cause you'll need to know, and it's all true, what I'll tell you, but none of it's official."

This brought a nod from Shade, then he glanced back to where the Mayor sat, his legs sedately crossed, his hands clasped in his lap, and his face swollen and colored like a hoodoo mask that kept children in line.

"I'm your man, Captain," he said and looked back at his superior. "What went down?"

"What went down is this." Bauer began to do some vaguely threatening theatrical business involving his squeezing rubber balls in both hands, on the desk top, so that his forearms twisted with cords of muscle. "Some of the finest money in this region was on one of the finest tables in this region and several gentlemen of the first rank were seated around that table along with a couple of ramblin', gamblin' colorful types who were there to add to the adventure and . . ."

"No sarcasm," the Mayor said in an atonal basso wheeze.

Bauer nodded grimly and went on.

". . . long about the witching hour three tough guys in ski masks come through the door. Can you fill in the rest yourself?"

Shade said, "The tough guys wanted that fine money and they had guns to take it with and Bell was the guard. Is that close?"

"Close enough. Bell was the guard, only he was also a bust-out gambler and pretty soon he was sittin' in on the game instead of watchin' the door for tough guys." Bauer really began to mash away at the rubber balls, his teeth grinding behind an open mouth. "See, Mr. B. has not been fucked with like this for a while, and everybody was gettin' lax. Now this has happened and everybody is pissed off and in kind of a spot."

"When Bell got shot," Shade said, "these pillar-of-the-community types who were there didn't want to be splattered by any shit, so they dumped the body at the hospital and called it a night, huh, Captain?"

"You got it," Bauer said.

"Who were they?" Shade asked. "I'd like to talk with them."

"I'm afraid that won't happen, Shade. I'm tellin' you all there is to tell, and it's all off the record." Bauer looked hard at Shade. "For the record Officer Bell died while off duty, probably in an attempt to halt a burglary."

"You think anybody'll buy that?"

From the shadowed corner came a flat, gasping answer. "It doesn't matter if it's believed or not," Mayor Crawford said. "It will wash."

"That's your opinion, Mayor."

"Yes, Detective Shade," the Mayor said, his voice thick with curdled civility. "It's only one man's opinion, but it's a man whose opinion means *just a little bit* in these parts."

Shade said, "You blew your nose, didn't you, Mayor?"

"Pardon?"

"One of these tough guys we been discussing belted you and your nose filled with blood and mucus, and your instinct was to blow it. So you did." Shade shook his head. "That's a case of an instinct misleading you, 'cause when you blow a busted beak it makes your eyes swell shut. Kind of like yours are."

"Why do you think I was there?"

"Because you're here."

Mayor Crawford was an almost unassailable political figure in St. Bruno. He had masterfully endeared himself to the rice-and-bean legions who all had one man, one vote, and he was personally liked for his roguish charm, his laissez-faire approach to victimless crime, and his poon-hound exploits as a tea-dance heart warper.

The Mayor now swiveled his gaze from Shade to Bauer, and nodded curtly.

"Okay," Bauer said, "it's like this, Shade. Our little metropolis is run by a certain system and now some fuckin' cowboys are throwin' shit in the gears. That's not good for anybody. Several factions in this town could run amuck if we don't step in and settle this."

"Uh-huh," Shade said. "Like some of your gambler pals, huh, Mayor?"

"Detective," the Mayor said, "be an adult—you'll always have a lot of gambling wherever you have a lot of blacks."

Shade laughed.

"Come on, all your gaming pals are white."

The Mayor sucked wind through his mouth.

"Them, too," he said.

At this moment, Shade was sensing a request that would be officially above and beyond the call, but unofficially crucial, and sweat slid down his temples. He wiped the sweat away, and said, "Christ, this'd be good weather to make weight in. What is it you want me to do?"

"Get the bastards," the Mayor said.

"That," Captain Bauer said, "and if possible save the taxpayers the expense of a trial."

The Captain's comment caused Shade to suddenly believe a legend, for there had long been one told about Bauer during last call at FOP meetings, and around anyplace cop buddies saluted their secret heroes, for this bit of law-and-order mythology claimed that the good Captain had performed just such an assignment years ago, when the Carpenter brothers had risen up and challenged Mr. B. It came about that the then Detective Bauer and his partner, Ervin Delahoussaye, had found themselves in a remote grain bin that was empty except for four spread-eagled Carpenters, only to have the brothers get allegedly combative and thereby cause their own deaths. Each brother, the coroner said, was shot twice in the head, and the whole thing was ruled justifiable force. Bauer leapfrogged up to captain, and cops young and old praised his marksmanship. Delahoussaye, clearly not leadership material, snacked on his gat six weeks later.

It was all true, Shade now knew, and he'd best step carefully.

"Are you telling me to take them off the count, Captain?"

"Not by yourself. There are other people who want to find these motherfuckers, too. One of them will help you."

"There may be some money in this," Mayor Crawford said. "A covert reward."

"No," Shade said, "I don't want money. I'm independently wealthy, anyhow. I mean, I've been poor so long it doesn't bother me anymore, and that's as much peace of mind as a Rockefeller's got." The sweat on his face again required mopping, then he asked, "Does it have to be me?"

"It does now," Bauer said. "Plus, our outside friends specifically asked for you."

"I see."

"Detective," the Mayor said and strolled toward him, "you've been around. You're from Frogtown—does this all seem too far out of the ordinary?"

"I can't call ordinary, Mayor. I can tell weird, but ordinary is a tough call to make." Shade bowed his head, trying hard to foresee all the angles, then raised his face and met the Captain's eyes. "Who am I supposed to work with?"

"Shuggie Zeck," Bauer said. "You're doing the right thing, Shade, in the long run. Shuggie's waiting for you now, at your brother's dive by the river, there, The Catfish Bar."

7

Over a bowl of guinea-hen gumbo, at a small white table in Maggie's Keyhole, Wanda Bone Bouvier was pressed into service as a luncheon audience of one for Hedda Zeck's slightly slurred tale of her past. As the ample Hedda, who disguised her ampleness behind a billow of yellow summer dress, told it, her life up 'til she hoisted this very bloody mary in her hand was a convoluted tale of bubbly love gone flat, fine talents unnoticed and similarly woeful bullshit.

"So," Hedda said, "Shuggie stands there, honey I mean he *stands* there like somebody who's got the fuckin' *right* to look at me that way, so evil, and he says, ''Til you sweat off some of that lard you're gonna have to bend like cookie dough and lick it your own self. You're only gonna get the ol' in-and-out until I see you in a dress that says size ten on it.'" Hedda sucked on her smoke, ignoring her own bowl of gumbo, shaking the ice cubes in her drink. "Would you take shit like that from a man, Wanda?"

"You're not fat, Hedda," Wanda said. "Besides, Shuggie ain't exactly a hunk hisself."

"He *is* chubby, isn't he?"

"He could sure enough stand to run some laps or something." Wanda had heard such miseries from Hedda before, but up until Ronnie had run afoul of Mr. B.'s organization it had mostly come out when the men had gotten up from the table and swaggered into a dark corner to talk business, as they put it. But now, with Ronnie an outcast from the group because he had gotten just a little too indiscriminating about whose money he hustled, they met only here, on the sly, out of the way. "You want another bloody mary?"

"Oh," Hedda said, "I shouldn't but I will." Hedda Zeck had been born a Langlois, which was a good thing to be in Frogtown since everyone knew they were cousins to the Beaurains, and she was ten years or so further down the track than Wanda. Her lips were full and red, and her hair was dark and cut short. Her twin vices were hard liquor and baked sweets, vices that greatly contributed to her dimensions, which in turn led to her being less often laid, which could possibly force her to acquire another vice that consisted of motel rooms and trampy men. "Aw, Wanda, wouldn't it be a nicer world if God just grinned and everybody got what they wanted?"

Wanda sipped her beer, shrugged and said, "I think that could get sort of boring, really."

"Honey," Hedda said and laughed, "I declare you'd find fault with the land of milk and honey."

"That's right," Wanda said. "You can't dream up a world I won't criticize."

They signaled for more drinks and got them, allowing the gumbo to cool until a film developed on top.

Wanda actually did like Hedda, and in more flush days she'd found the older woman to be of some use in the selection of clothing, furniture, vacations and other matters that didn't mean squat since they got mad and fed Ronnie to the law. She'd had to sell off everything to pay lawyers and landlords. The high life had been snatched back away from her and here she was, in cutoff jeans, sandals, and a cheap cotton shirt with Technicolor vegetation on it, listening to a gal with a few wads in her wallet rambling on about the hardships in this torture called *her* life.

"Hedda," Wanda said, "I wish Auguste and Shuggie and them'd quit bad-mouthin' Ronnie all over town. These things get back to me sometimes and it don't make me feel too good." Wanda took a big gulp of her beer and gestured for another since she knew who'd pick up the tab. "I mean, they done run our name down to the goddam dogs. I'll admit Ronnie misbehaved. I admit that."

"Honey," Hedda said, squinting through a puff of smoke, "he cheated Auguste."

"Aw, Hedda, really now, that was just sort of an in-joke that got out. He was just seein' if he could do it, as, like, a security check."

"He took bets on races that were already run, honey. Auguste considers that cheating."

"Now, Hedda, come on," Wanda said. She stared sullenly into her mug of beer. "I bet there ain't a bookie south of Minneapolis who ain't took a post bet or some such shenanigans just to make ends meet once in a while."

Another beer arrived, along with an unrequested bloody mary that Hedda decided not to send back.

"Wanda," she said with a vodka stumble in her voice, "people get killed for what Ronnie done. I *love* you, honey. I *love* you like a little sister, and I screamed and screamed when that all came up, but if I wasn't kin of the Beaurains I think you'd've been wearin' *bl-ack* for a while."

"I know you went out on a limb," Wanda said.

"But I don't mind," Hedda said. "I *love* you."

Up at the bar a middle-aged woman with one leg, her crutches leaning against the rail beside her, did a merry-go-round number on her stool, spinning slowly enough that the I Can't Help It If I'm Lucky on her T-shirt could be read. Behind the bar a preened man in a brewery uniform was loading beer into the coolers, his gaze frequently circling around Wanda's way, as if he was hoping that regular blasts from his icy blues would prompt some spur-of-the-moment afternoon lushness to come into his arms.

The third time Wanda caught his Nordic Casanova act she flipped him the bird and he kept his eyes on business.

If this tête-à-tête had been strictly for friendship Wanda would've gladly gone awash on draft, but there were things that she needed to know and Hedda was her only source. The bloody marys were providing an assist, and Hedda seemed primed.

Wanda put some zippidy-doo-dah into her smile, and said, "But what else is new with you?"

"It's none of it new," Hedda answered, using both hands to tame the wobbling of her drink. "I hardly get to shop. Shuggie won't leave me the checkbook since, you know, since I like nice things and checks can be traced, right, traced and then added up by the tax man. The fuckin' tax man has ruined my life, 'cause now I gotta use cash and I gotta wait for fat-assed Shuggie to give it to me." She looked blearily at her audience. "Ain't I half of this marriage?"

"At least," Wanda said.

"He used to say for me to use good judgment, but now he just says forget it, no way."

"I'm sure he's busy nowadays," Wanda said amiably. "Tryin' to oversee all of Auguste's games and other interests. Crime is a job, when you get right up against it."

"Tell me about it. It's like a doctor, like Shuggie's an odd sort of doctor or something, the way they call any hour of the night. Like last night, it must've been, I don't know, late. Real late. I don't remember what time, but it was late, 'cause I was asleep and the TV was all static, and they called." Hedda fumbled for a cigarette, then lit it. "Some problem at the country club, they had some kind of uppity poker game or somethin'. Some problem, I don't know. They call anytime, day or night."

"Well, Shuggie can handle any problems," Wanda said. "He'll probably have it straightened out by now."

"Prob'ly. He ain't come home yet, when I left. He called. He's a good li'l boy that way, he calls home and tells me where he's at. It's in case he gets murdered, I think, so I'll know who to sick Auguste on." Hedda leaned toward Wanda, drunkenly sincere. "Do you think Ronnie fucked aroun' on you? Do you?"

"Not tremendously."

"But some?"

"I imagine. I mean, I'd eat a tame man up, and I couldn't eat him up."

"Does Shuggie fuck around?"

"I doubt it. He never came on to me, Hedda. I'd tell you if he did."

"You're a dear, you know it?" Hedda waved her cigarette around, and picked at some tomato juice that had slopped onto her summer dress and dried. "That makes me feel better about him and all them naked girls out there."

"Out where?"

"When he called he said to send messages out there to that place, you know, on River Road? Where them naked girls dance and bend over with their tushes in men's faces, trollin' for dollar bills to be stuffed in their garters."

"Huh," Wanda said.

"We went once, me and Shuggie, just for the hell of it. It didn't help." Hedda was swaying in her chair, becoming dangerous with the hot end of her smoke. "I imagine he's openin' a game there, or somethin', after that trouble last night."

"Is that The Rio, Rio Club?" Wanda asked.

"That's it. They wax their pussy hairs out there. I *saw*."

"Listen, Hedda, I got to get goin'," Wanda said. She stood, came around the table, and embraced her friend and unknowing informant. "I'll call you a cab, okay?"

"Ooh, I *love* you."

As Wanda pulled into her dirt-rut driveway she saw the men's car parked back behind the bougainvillea at the side of the house. When she came in the front door she heard a muffled pop and some hairy-chested guffaws.

She went into the sparsely furnished family room and immediately noticed a couple of dozen eraser-sized holes punched in the walls near the floor.

"What on earth?" she said, then looked closer and saw unshelled peanuts littered about. She heard the guffaws again and tracked the source to the side porch where she found Dean and Cecil in *her* underwear, waving Ronnie's pellet rifle around. "You fuckin' slobs," she said.

"Uh-oh," Dean said with a drunken smile, "the land-lady's home."

Wanda extracted a recitation of the chain of events from Cecil and found that it all started when Emil went back to bed and Cecil decided to flaunt his worldliness by mixing up a batch of gimlets, four parts gin to a teaspoon of lime juice, the way muckety-mucks mix it in Clear-water, Florida, a place where he'd once had a bartender buddy. Anyhow, Wanda learned, you got to give the snooty sorts a tip of the cap on this, 'cause it's a flat-out monster drink and Dean, you know, Dean lets himself into your bedroom looking for a Band-Aid for the finger he cut after he'd dropped the first pitcher, that glass one with the fancy scenes painted on it, and down there in your closet where you keep a bunch of crotchless panties and negligees in that oatmeal box, you know, down there, he turns up this here pellet gun and says he can shoot bet-ter'n me. I told him I could hit an unshelled peanut from across the room, and, by golly, two or three times I did.

"Oh, man," Wanda said disgustedly when the whole thing had been run down to her. She looked at them as they hoisted their gimlets in green plastic cups, Dean in a pair of lavender French-cut panties, and Cecil in a pink pair with a red zipper down the middle she'd gotten mail-order. "You fellas go on and just *keep* them panties, hear? My treat."

Wanda's presence seemed to bring the fun buddies down, and pretty soon she got the gun away from them and they turned the TV on and cuddled up to get *au courant* with some soaps they'd missed since Braxton. Wanda went into the kitchen and Jadick came out of the bedroom in his pants, but shirtless.

She fixed him with a baleful gaze and said, "I hope to god the FBI ain't buggin' this house, Emil. They'll ridicule us in court."

"Bad day?" he asked.

He went to the kitchen sink and splashed water on his face.

"I found out what you wanted," she said. "Hedda was half lit when I got there."

"Oh, yeah?" Jadick said, suddenly intent. He held a dish towel at his face, poised to dry it. "Where?"

Wanda took a seat at the table and began to stack all of the empty beer cans.

"A tits and ass dance joint out on River Road."

"Is it Beaurain's?"

"I imagine, it's out this side of town."

"Hmm," Jadick went, and sat down across the table. "So there's liable to be a bunch of wise guys in there. That could be a problem if we come on too loose."

"I don't know about those things," Wanda said. Looking through the litter on her own kitchen table she turned up half a doobie and put fire to it. As she choked out a deep toke she asked, "You always been a stickup guy? Or have you did different things?"

Jadick smiled, and it was a shockingly pleasant, white-toothed smile. He held a finger to a flat part of his nose.

"I used to be a fighter," he said.

"Before you were a stickup guy?"

"Kind of in between," he said. "This was some years back, in Philadelphia. I had moved there to be a fighter, plus I was drawin' some heat in Cleveland. I knocked a grown man out with one punch when I was thirteen, so I always held it in the back of my mind that I could have a career down that line. So I went to Philly, and all

66

these experts said a white dude couldn't stand up under all the shit they'd dish out in that bad town. But I didn't listen and became a sparring partner, which is to say a punching bag. They were all the time poundin' me 'cause I'd never had formal lessons or nothin', just instinct and a wallop." He shook his head wistfully. "Pun-kin, them niggers zapped my eyes shut, and never even sprang for a soda, just beat on me and said, 'Can't take it, can you, ofay?'"

"What'd you do?"

"I went back to the stickup dodge, gorilla work. I won't tolerate that shit from niggers. Fightin' niggers is like dancin' with a pig, anyhow, it ain't meant to be."

"That's a shame," she said. "You got a plan for The Rio, Rio Club? That's where the game'll be."

"I'll think about it."

"Well," Wanda said, "I was fixin' to intrude an idea of my own on you. See, the boy across the street works there. He's older'n me, really, so I shouldn't call him boy, but he gets a tent in his britches every time he sees me. I reckon he'd show me a good time out there if I acted interested."

"When could you do that?"

"Tomorrow. He's already there by now."

"No," Jadick said. "We'd have to cap him, then, or he'd snap to it after the rip. No." He leaned across the table and patted her hand. "I think you should go out there right away and apply for a job. I want to hit them tonight."

"Tonight? Tonight? Man, your gang is in the other room too drunk to wear men's clothes!"

"Nah, I can sober 'em up." Jadick stood and walked to the fridge. "If we hit 'em again tonight I think they'll be sort of freaked out, ready to fall."

"Emil, I'm no stripper."

"You got the raw talent," he said. "Just juggle it around."

The phone was on the wall by the fridge. When it rang Jadick answered it, listened for a moment, then said, "Yeah, we'll accept charges." He turned to Wanda. "It's Ronnie."

"You shouldn't be answering my phone," Wanda said. She took the phone from Emil and cradled it to her ear. "Hello, Ronnie. What? Yeah, that was him. He's here. Your relatives are here." She leaned against the fridge and watched Emil. "You heard that already? Up there? He was a what? What? Oh, man." She held the phone down and said, "That was a cop, Emil. You all killed a cop."

Emil shrugged and opened the refrigerator and took out a carton of milk. "Life goes on," he said.

"Yes, Ronnie. Of course, yeah. I'm a little worried now. Naturally I am. Uh-huh, I know I have to be strong. I understand."

Wanda hated the picture of her legal lover man she had in her mind, for she thought of him as jailhouse pale, chain-smoking Luckies, dressed in that bright white target uniform they wore at Braxton. She had this sad image of him at the same time Emil stood before her drinking milk straight from the carton, his stomach all muscled and firm, crying out for her fingertips to be stroked down it to the happy stick.

"You know I do, Ronnie. You know I love you. Uh-huh. I did what you told me." She began to twirl the phone cord around her fingers as Emil locked his eyes on hers. "Uh-huh, you told me I should. Well, that's why I did. Ronnie, I ain't going to lie to you: I dug it. He's younger'n you. You know he's real built, big arms and all."

Jadick, realizing that he was under discussion, fell back

against the kitchen counter, his legs spread, his chest puffed.

Wanda could not take her eyes off him.

"Uh-huh, Ronnie, yes. I'll do what he wants because it's for you, really, it's for you. Everything I do is for you. Uh-huh. Okay, I do like him. Well, you know," she said, her eyes going to Emil's, "he's a little bit sentimental and a little bit mean: in other words, just right. Okay, Ronnie. You know I love you and that's no shit, neither, baby." She hung up the phone and sighed.

"He says to go on, keep doing what you need."

"I knew he would," Jadick said. "Ronnie knows what it takes, pun-kin. Not everybody does."

"Uh-huh." Wanda felt flushed by the conversation and the manly aroma of a sweaty Jadick. "Let's don't kid each other," she said, "the bedroom's thisaway."

Jadick laughed and took her by the arm in a nearly courtly manner.

"There you go," he said. "I'll get you good and limber for your audition, pun-kin."

8

The Catfish Bar was on Lafitte Street, the main artery of Frogtown, a short stroll from Shade's apartment. He left his car at home and took the railroad-track route, the back way to the bar. He passed two old men who were hauling a stringer of channel cat home from a slough, and a smattering of drunks dozing it off in the sun. Up the tracks at the bridge he saw a group of neighborhood lads, neophyte sadists in dirty Air Jordan sneakers and fresh scowls, prowling for ethnic winos or solvent strangers to ratpack. As he reached the dirt alley beside The Catfish he passed a young man and a mature woman sitting in a candy-colored four-barrel muscle car, friskily familiarizing themselves with each other's anatomy.

The Catfish was a place of raw wood and a colorful past, the chief neighborhood rendezvous for as long as Shade could remember. His grandfather Blanqui had hung out here when the floors were sawdusted, free lunches did exist, and the Kingfish was everybody's hero. Little had changed over the years except ownership, and that had passed into the hands of Shade's older brother, Tip.

When Shade came into the bar Shuggie Zeck was sitting on a barstool talking to Tip. They both turned toward the sunlight that came in the open door.

"Well, well," Shade said, "I'll be dogged if it ain't Joe Shit, the ragman, live and in person." He sat on a stool twice removed from Shuggie. "How you hanging?"

"You talkin' to me?" Shuggie asked. "I don't believe you're talkin' to *me* like that."

"Believe," Shade said. He nodded then at his brother. Tip was an up-and-down sibling, into a lot of secret this-and-that, and the brothers were not close. "You're looking good, Tip."

"Hey, you, too, li'l blood."

Tip Shade was large and pock-faced with a heavy dose of the sullens and long brown hair.

"I'm the one you're here to see," Shuggie said. Shuggie was a hybrid of flab and flash, who, try as he would to upscale his image, could not groom himself past looking like six feet of Frogtown funneled into pinstripes. He had a Lafitte Street yen for gaudy rings and wore two to a hand. His hair was dark and curly and his face was like that of a bulldog who smiled easily. "We're goin' to be pals, right, Rene? Like the old days, huh? Remember the old days?"

"Yeah, I remember," Shade said. "Every time I look into the holding tank."

Shade and Shuggie had shared an inkish youth, an adolescence given over to the moiling passions of white-trash teens, and on nights fueled by fear and anger, pride and chance, they had done many things criminal and a few

71

just plain mean. As serendipity would have it, Shade escaped charges on all counts, was only stomped by cops once, and outgrew his criminal aspects when he devoted himself to boxing. Over his sporting years Shade drifted apart from Shuggie and Tip and a street-corner choir of other accomplices. He had since endeavored to go down that endless crooked road that was somehow misnamed the straight and narrow.

"Want a beer?" Tip asked.

"Sure. Très bien, big bro." Shade reached into his pocket and pulled out the black beauty cached in the Alka-Seltzer foil, and popped it into his mouth. Tip handed him a draw in a mug and he took a swallow. "Merci."

"What was that you just ate?" Shuggie asked.

"Sinus tablet," Shade said. "This humidity. So, Shuggie, let's get it right straight from the giddy-up— I'm going along with you as long as it seems to be going somewhere."

"I'll be going somewhere, all right." Shuggie smiled and beckoned to Tip. "Tell your hard-on brother what you seen over at Frechette Park, Tippy. Tell him where I'm takin' him."

"Well," Tip said, and leaned against the bar, his massive arms folded, "I was over there in the park, there, Rene, up above Bum's Hollow, there, and at a picnic table I seen Bobby Gillette and two other fellas. This was yesterday, and they were all huddled together, you know, fomentin' something for sure."

"Bobby Gillette, huh?" Shade said. "Who the fuck is Bobby Gillette?"

"He's a fella who never learns," Tip said. "That's what

I'm tellin' you, I know the dude, and he never learns."

"There's a lot of that going around," Shade said.

"Hey look, don't you remember?" Shuggie asked. "A couple of years ago? You don't? Well, Bobby Gillette was the one who knocked over a game Delbert McKechnie had, then he did one on me. He's a tush hog, lives out in the country, on a spit of soggy dirt out there called Gumbo. Know the place?"

"I've been by there."

"Back then, Mr. B. was worried about Mayor Gene's election that was comin' up, so we had to play it smart. So Gerry Bell ended up nailin' Gillette in the act of a burglary he never heard of, but the beef stood up in court." Shuggie sipped from his own drink, his pinkie rings bright in the tavern gloom. "Tough guy did a bit on Trahan's Farm, got out a month ago."

"I never heard about those games being hit," Shade said. "I never heard a thing."

"That's the price you pay for bein' standoffish," Shuggie said. He spun on his stool to face Shade. "If you were still my friend you'd hear things like that."

"I'm sure I'd hear things all right."

"If we were friends you'd hear the *right* things, Rene."

"You don't know any right things, Shuggie."

"Jerk," Shuggie said. Shuggie Zeck, who considered himself to embody the Horatio Alger myth, if Horatio had been as wise to the angles and had his connections, but who did not feel that ambition necessarily required deceit, said, "Did I ever lie to you? *Ever?*"

Shade, whose sense of trust had been badly singed by experience, sucked down some suds, then said, "That time we stole four cases of Old Grandad from Langlois'

73

Liquor and hid them under the bridge you did. You said somebody else ripped it from us, but I always have figured you beat me out of it."

"Jesus," Shuggie said with a wince, "that's really goin' back there, man. But I told you the real deal then, and I'd tell it to you now, once in a while, if we were friends."

"I'd come in handier than Officer Bell, huh, Shuggie?"

"I doubt that," Shuggie said. "Bell had motivation, and you don't seem to."

"I seen a good ball game up in St. Louie," Tip said out of the blue. "Jack Clark belted one I just missed by two rows."

"I'll never work for you, Shuggie."

"Ah, you don't want to 'cause you know me and familiarity breeds contempt."

"Familiarity with *you* certainly does."

"Clark is the best power hitter they've had since Stan the Man if you ask me."

"Fuck you, Shade."

"Fuck *with* me, Zeck."

"Give him a heater on the inside of the plate and somebody gets a free ball in the cheap seats." Tip suddenly slammed a palm on the bar, the boom startling even the drunks nodding in the far corners of the room. "Shuggie," big Tip said, "this is my li'l blood, Rene. Now, Rene, you li'l piglet, you, this is Shuggie. You two start over from scratch, huh? What's buried in the past is dead and already returned to nature, such as shit does. If I was you fellas I'd be friendly first; then, if and when that don't work no more, then go ahead, what the fuck, settle it at Knuckle Junction."

One of the drunks who'd been startled awake by Tip's conciliatory boom began to sing some crazed gimmick song from way back that claimed the singer was entangled by incest and was in fact his own grandpa. His drinking buddy shooshed him but made no effort to leave, and soon joined in on the sad family refrain.

"Come on," Shuggie said. "Tippy's right. Let's go, there's somebody who wants to meet you who I think you ought to meet."

"As long as it goes somewhere," Shade said. He then patted his brother's shoulder and asked him, "If I wasn't with Zeck would you've told me about Bobby Gillette?"

"You know I wouldn't, Rene," Tip said. "It wouldn't really be the right move for me if you think about it."

"I knew that," Shade said as he followed Shuggie to the door. "I just wanted to be reminded."

9

As the sliding doors to the pool area were opened and Shade and Shuggie entered, a loud voice was raised: "Solve the riddle! Solve the riddle! Don't spin the wheel, Miss Greedy, solve the riddle!"

Auguste Beaurain sat at poolside on a wicker chair that had Tahitian pretensions but had been made in Memphis, watching a game show. The swimming pool was enclosed by glass, roofed with same, and plants of several sizes were growing from pots on the parquet floor. Beaurain wore a white suit with a blue shirt and a jaunty yellow tie. The pool was calm and empty and the air conditioner was on.

"Afternoon, Mr. Beaurain," Shuggie said. "This is Rene Shade."

"I know," Beaurain said. He did not take his eyes from the TV until the contestant went bust, then he growled, "Greedy people get what they deserve *sometimes*." He then snapped the TV set off and said, "Detective Shade, do you understand the world you live in?"

"Which part of it?" Shade asked.

"The whole of it."

"No, I don't. And neither do you." Shade sat down on a nearby chair and set his feet on a small, glass-topped table, thereby establishing his insolence. "Mind if I sit?"

"Of course not." Beaurain lifted a bowl of nuts and held it toward Shade. "Help yourself. I particularly like the cashews, myself. I'd appreciate it if you left them for me."

"No thanks."

"Okay." Beaurain set the bowl down. "Shuggie, sit, be comfortable." Beaurain measured five foot seven standing on your neck. He had a lean but lined face, with a pleasant arrangement of features, and a nearly constant smile. His hair was gray, thin, and carefully combed. He had all the attributes of a "Disney Hour" grandpappy but his was in fact the whip hand held over the insolvent and indictable of St. Bruno. "We've met before," he said to Shade. "Twice. Once when you were a small boy. Your daddy is John X. Shade, isn't it? You were with him, years ago. There were three of you boys, one not so little. Your daddy used to book bets for me, Detective."

"He ever give you a short count and lam out on you?"

"No, he never did."

"Then it must've been a different John X. Shade, Mr. B."

"You really *don't* understand the world you live in, do you? Ah"—Beaurain shook his head like a displeased schoolteacher—"that will make this harder."

"He's a knucklehead," Shuggie said. "I've known him since we had to stand on a bicycle seat to sneak through a window."

"You told me that," Beaurain said.

"You said twice," Shade drawled. "When was the other

77

time we met? I don't remember it. I've seen you around, but I don't remember meeting you."

"Well, you were sort of distracted the second time. The first time you were a child and the second time you'd just encountered Foster Broome in your one chance at the title. I'm not certain you could even see, your eyes looked like tomatoes squashed on cement." Beaurain laughed. "That nigger whupped you like he'd caught you stealing chickens, didn't he?"

"He was a great fighter," Shade said. "I was offered a shot at him so I took it and he kicked my ass. Big deal."

"I knew you'd take the fight," Beaurain said. He extracted a cashew from the bowl and ate it. "And I knew you'd lose."

"What do you mean, you knew?"

Beaurain laughed and said to Shuggie, "He really is a knucklehead, ain't he?" He then turned to Shade, looking disgusted. "How do you think you got that fight, asshole? Your record was what—eighteen and seven?"

"Eighteen and six at the time," Shade said. "I ended up twenty-four and nine."

"Whatever. I put up the guarantee for that fight, Detective. I wanted to see a local boy get a chance at the big brass ring. I guaranteed Broome's purse so you could get it."

"Why?" Shade pulled his feet off of the table and sat up straight. There was nothing insolent about him now, and he needed to know more. "Why would you do that?"

"Like I said, I knew you'd lose. But I remembered your daddy, and I always liked him, and I knew every redneck, half a wise guy, and straight citizen from this town would bet on you. It got even better when the niggers went for you, too. That surprised me, but they bet you probably, oh, sixty percent. Go figure, you see. That's why it's called gambling."

"Well, I came through for you," Shade said. "I lost."

"Yes, but you were given a chance. I want you to note this, too. It wasn't the nuns at St. Peter's who got it for you. It wasn't a group of lawyers, judges, doctors and poets who got it for you. No, Shade, there was not a consortium of moneyed saints and sporting bankers from Hawthorne Hills interested in seeing a Frogtown boy like you get a chance to punch out a place in history. No," Beaurain said with a slow head shake, "the good people of St. Bruno stood apart from you, but I didn't."

This was all news to Shade, and it went back to a not so distant phase of his life when he'd been on the cusp of both worlds, straddling the street and the straight and narrow, and it was the fact that he'd actually, miraculously, been given a title shot that had convinced him that the world was benign more often than he'd given it credit for. He was not old now by any calculations other than the athletic, but he suddenly felt like an ancient dupe, a moron, a man who couldn't tell fresh creamy butter from pig fat.

"I hear you," he said, "but I don't think I owe you shit."

"Oh, no, you don't owe me anything. I'm just helping you toward understanding the world you live in." Beaurain clapped his hands and said, "Norman, bring us some drinks!"

A pale, round-faced man came out from behind a green curtain of plants. He was bald and wore a shoulder holster.

"Who's that?" Shade asked.

79

"That's my son-in-law, Norman the Jew. He watches over me here, him and my daughter. This is a bad neighborhood, you know."

All of the men chuckled, for none of them had ever willingly lived anywhere else. Beaurain's house was very modest when viewed from the street, but the interior was richly furnished, and he'd added on the pool room in back. He had the down payment for a palace anywhere but he stayed here, in Frogtown, not two full blocks from the house he'd been born in.

Presently, Norman came back carrying a tray of drinks. He set the tray on the table and went silently back to his sniper blind behind the plants.

"I only drink tonic water in summer," Beaurain said. "The quinine, you know."

Shade was feeling the first tingling waves of illegal alertness. He lifted a glass and gulped from it.

"You ever been arrested?" he asked. "I heard we've never popped you for anything."

"That's right," Beaurain said. "I'll go to heaven. My record is free of criminal charges."

"That's amazing."

"Well, I'm a likable person, Shade. People seem to want to be nice to me. Plus, I'm not greedy, so I don't make enemies the way you'd expect."

Mr. B.'s rep, though clangorous and fearful, was, Shade knew, that he was a fair-minded breed of gangster. Street slime and sly businessmen considered him to be more decisive than the legal system, a good deal more fair, but when he convicted someone his sentences tended to be forty-five caliber.

"Maybe I'll nail you," Shade said. His teeth were grinding and he had a black-beauty sense of optimism.

"Jerk," Shuggie said.

"What would be the point?" Beaurain asked. "I'm a good governor. Let me tell you, Detective. Let me tell you about greed, which I don't have. Down on the south side here, there's Del McKechnie and Benny Kreuger and Georgie Sedillo, and, oh, one or two others. Do I fuck with them? Do I make life a heartache for them? No. No, maybe I accept a tithe, presents really, when they offer them to me, which is, frankly, always. Do I want more? Do I want it all? No, that'd be greedy. Greed makes trouble. So I accept a tithe and things go smooth. And over in Pan Fry Mr. Sundown Phillips has things pretty much under control but, still, I know people he doesn't and maybe he gives me a piece, a small percentage, out of respect. I accept graciously. I don't send Shuggie over there to make trouble, and I don't let Rudy Regot or Steve Roque or any of the Frogtown cliques go into the south side and come on rugged with the fellas down there."

"Yeah," Shade said, "and does everybody live happily ever after?"

"Jerk."

"Shade," Beaurain said, "if you weren't a cop, what would you be?"

"I might be you."

"Never, never, you don't even understand the world you live in, how could you be me?"

"I could dress spiffy and talk like a duke, too, if it wasn't that I'd rather wear rags and feel free to spit on dukes."

"I'm sorry, Mr. Beaurain," Shuggie said. "This is how he always is."

"Oh, don't be sorry," Beaurain said. He ferreted out another cashew and put it in his mouth, then sucked on it behind a smile. "He's what you said he'd be. Shade, I wonder, are you a good Christian?"

"My case is under review."

"Ah, but I think you want to be. I admire that. The higher-calling angle, you see, can inspire men toward greatness. It can also delude them. Ponder it." Beaurain hunched forward, his hands on his knees. "I'm glad to have met you. But now is business. As you know there are some ruffians going around, hurting people, fucking things up. They're greedy, they're stupid, they're going to pay. Your team feels the same as my team, Detective, and it's all of us against the umpires."

"So I was told," Shade said. "I'm not a fuckin' hit man, though."

"Jerk."

"Shuggie, you call me a jerk again and I'm gonna kick your fat ass in front of your boss."

"Come on *with it*, Rene."

"Shut up," Beaurain said with a wince of offended elegance. "Both of you. I feel like I'm a kid again, with all this fistfighting shit, and, believe me, my kid years are *not* my favorite memory." Beaurain looked over his shoulder toward the gun position behind the petunias. "Norman, show these gents the door." He then quickly spun back to Shade. "I don't want to see you get hurt, Detective Shade, but you don't know enough about the world you live in. I could tell you, but I don't have time."

Shade stood and shook his legs loose and felt the pleasant amphetamine back beat of his heart.

"They whacked one of ours, Mr. B., and I'm in it because of that. But later, I might get on you just to see your moves." Shade extended his hand to the overlord of his town.

"Very well. Bonne chance. I look forward to it." Beaurain stood and shook Shade's hand. "Just remember the birds-and-bees of business—I fuck you or you fuck me. And there aren't many birthday parties for fellas who've fucked me."

Shade smiled widely and stared hard into Beaurain's face.

"You talk a lot of shit about knowing the world we live in, Mr. B., but you're dangerously fuckin' confused about me. I want you to know that up-front."

≡ **10** ≡

As it had been on so many key days in Wanda Bone
Bouvier's life, the sky above her head was murky, backed
up by soiled wads of cloud. She drove west from home
looking for a through street to the north. A smoking stick
of boo was in her left hand, clasped to the steering wheel.
Her right hand held a bottle of Pepsi that she'd clogged
with salted peanuts and called a late lunch.

She hit River Road and jumped on the gas, prompting
gut checks in oncoming motorists when she passed the
old pokies in her path. She sucked on the doobie,
chomped and swished her southland snack, speeding on
by a seedy stretch of small businesses and stores where
the cashiers tended to keep their hands beneath the counter when strangers came in.

It was a gray, hot, horsefly afternoon, and her skin felt
slick with sweat when she pulled into the parking lot of
The Rio, Rio Club. The joint was a large prefab aluminum concoction, guaranteed to go south in a heavy wind,
with a sign above the door that said, BUSCH ON TAP,
ROOMS TO LET.

Wanda had pondered several themes she might embody and had opted to attempt the fresh-out-of-high-school-but-willing approach. She wore a pale green and yellow summer dress, with fifty cents' worth of pearls around her neck, red lipstick and yellow spike heels. When she came in the club she saw a round stage with a light above it, and a woman lying on a blanket doing splits. Jerry Lee Lewis, a regional hero, was booming from the speakers, "The Killer" singing a vigorously sad song about bad love gone worse, and beating his piano like he was married to it.

Wanda took a seat up against the stage and studied the bare gal's performance. The audience was a steamy-eyed group therapy conglomeration of night-shift factory drones, expense account raconteurs and countrified shy guys. The dancer did her limber thing lying on a pink blanket, seemingly unaware that others were in the room, doing her gynecologically revealing calisthenics as if she were at home with the curtains drawn.

Wanda looked into the supine dancer's eyes and decided that the woman seemed so aloof because she *was* aloof, likely hiding behind a reds and daiquiri veil.

"What'll you have, sister?" the bartender asked.

"A glass of whatever's on tap."

The bartender was a husky old hustler, in a nice white shirt with a red bow tie. When he set the beer in front of Wanda he said, "Pardon me for askin', ma'am, but are you a dyke?"

"Does it matter?"

"It'd break my heart."

"I'm just watchin' her out of boredom—my TV's on the fritz." Wanda tasted the beer. "Mmm, good'n cold. Leon around?"

"Leon? Leon?" The bartender did a mock stagger, his

hand over his heart. "You ain't gonna stop 'til you *do* break it, are you?"

Wanda dealt the old boy a smile as a reward for still having the pluck to try.

"He's just a friend," Wanda said, coyly smiling, her eyes angled down demurely. "I only fuck elderly bartenders. Is he here?"

"Elderly? Girl, you are flat-out cruel." The bartender pointed to a loft ten feet above the front door where audio equipment was set up. "He's somewhere in there, honey. He spins the records. He'll be done after this tune for the girl's break."

As she waited for the music to end Wanda scanned The Rio, Rio Club, furtively memorizing the layout. Basically, it was a barn, with only one interesting door, back in the left rear. She thought she heard a hammer over the blues, then the music was gone and she knew she did. There was some hammering being done, back behind the interesting door.

"Hey, Wanda, I saw you come in," Leon Roe said. He sat on the stool next to her. "Want a beer? I can get you a free one."

"I got one."

"I'll make it free for you."

"Thanks, Leon."

Leon had a narrow face, with a shiny forehead perfectly halved by a well-trained spit curl. He had a hesitant way about him but he dressed like a cowpoke star who wanted to pull in a more fashion-conscious crowd. There was black piping on his lavender western-cut coat, and his eggshell shirt was capped off by a blue string tie held up by a turquoise clasp that resembled an extra-large spider. At some recent time he'd spent too much on a pair of rattlesnake boots, and he wore one of those silver belt buckles that made a statement about his favorite brand of beer.

"Well," he said, his cheeks flushing, "what you been doing?"

"Anything, and a lot of it," Wanda said.

"Oh," Leon said, smiling. He found her to have a rare, exciting psychology, and he watched her now, as always, with an expression of nose-to-the-glass fascination. "Ever been here before?"

"No. It looks sort of cheap."

"Uh-huh," Leon said, "I agree, see, but, you know, I'm only here for the experience. To learn the entertainment business."

"You call this the entertainment business?"

"I call it a start, the first step. Elvis once drove a truck."

Wanda noticed a few workmen coming out of the door that concerned her. She turned to Leon and put her hand on his thigh.

"I need a job," she said, staring him into a puddle. "Could you help?"

"Here? You mean, here, Wanda? I'll loan you some money," he said. "We *are* neighbors. That means something to me."

"I'd rather earn it."

Leon studied the toes of his snakeskins.

"This place is total nudity," he said. "Some of the stuff gets pretty tasteless."

"I noticed," Wanda said. "I'd bring up the level, I reckon. Don't you think I'd look pretty classy in the buff, Leon?"

"Oh, God," he said, "I think you probably look too classy, too fine, for a place like this."

She patted his thigh, her hand lightly, nearly accidentally brushing his crotch. He was so easy to play, she thought, sadly out of place in the nighthawk realm. The kind of guy who walked down Seventh Street in broad daylight and prompted muggers to look up and say "Bingo!"

"Leon, why don't you find your boss and let *him* decide if he can use a fresh face? Won't you do that for me, sweetheart?"

Leon ushered Wanda into the room behind the interesting door, and introduced her to Fat Frank Pischelle. He sat at a small table, hunkered over a plate of chili dogs. His black hair was swept straight back and he sported a long goatee with dangling streaks of gray.

"You ever done this before?" he asked.

"Sort of. At a party or two," Wanda said. Fat Frank's fatness was vaguely nauseating at this distance. "But never what you'd call professional."

"We strip to the crack here," Fat Frank said. "Are you sure you're up for something that new and different?"

Wanda jutted her hips and smirked.

"Mister," she said, "I bust a cherry every day gettin' some new kind of kick."

"I'll bet that's true," he said. He used a fork to chop off a mouthful of chili dog, then sat back and stared at her while he chewed.

Wanda spun on her spikes, slowly spinning so that her selling points were highlighted, and as she did this modeling turn her eyes took in the two poker tables and the craps box, the exit door in the southwest corner, and the shotgun perch that had been built up on the wall. She put her hands on her hips and went into that salesmanship spin again.

"I'm an interesting thing if you look at me," she said. "My figure's nice. I play basketball like a man so you won't find no cottage cheese on my butt. No sir," she said and patted her haunches, "this little fanny is harder'n married life."

Fat Frank's attention was split between the chili dogs and Wanda. His expression was dispassionate, cool and almost bored. He took in another bite of his meal that would've put two jockeys out of work.

"You gotta audition," he said. "Leon, put a quarter in the juke over there."

Leon was sweaty-faced and pale, silently pledging allegiance to Cupid, for his dreams were being answered. He gave Wanda a thumbs up and walked to the jukebox.

"What should I play?"

"A-seven," Fat Frank said from behind a mouthful. He pointed at Wanda, wagging his finger until he'd swallowed. "That's 'Love Potion Number Nine,' honey. I use the same song on everybody 'cause everybody knows it." He picked up a napkin and daintily dabbed at his mouth, then clasped his hands on the tabletop. "Let's see your version."

In the brief moment before the song began Wanda decided she'd improvise a narrative strip, an impromptu skin story with plenty of tits and ass to hold her audience. As the tune boomed she went with the lyrics, holding her nose between two fingers, closing her eyes dramatically, then mimed taking a drink. She hopped about on her high heels a little awkwardly through the part where she wasn't supposed to know if it was day or night, doing a wicked imitation of stunned innocence as she kissed everything in sight, and she loosened her dress and let it slide, slide, slide when she acted out kissing the wrong cop on Thirty-fourth and Vine, and her breasts were bared, revealing pink nipples the size of peach halves, then she kicked free of the folds, baring herself down to spikes, pearls, and red G-string panties, and bent over with her ass aimed at Fat Frank, her eyes on Leon, and she shook, shook, shook from side to side, then front to back in a crowd-pleasing mimicry of the thrusting arts, until the cop broke that little bottle of Love Potion Number Nine. She ended her recital standing straight, a hand on either side of her open mouth, in a wide-eyed gesture of surprise.

The song ended and she dropped her hands to her hips.

"Well?" she asked.

Fat Frank nodded slowly and said, "Corny interpretation, but lots of verve. I can use you starting a week from Friday. What's your name?"

"How about Sinful Cindy?"

"Naw. We already got a Sinful Suzie." Fat Frank raised his fork. "How about Moaning Lisa?"

Wanda shrugged.

"Kind of artsy, ain't it?"

Fat Frank nodded, then drove the fork deeper into the chili.

"That's the secret me," he said. "My face fools people. Leon, explain things to her, somewhere else. This is my mealtime."

Wanda picked up the wadded dress, then followed Leon back to the front room, her heels clicking on the cement. She went to the bar, naked still, and lifted her beer for a drink. The bartender stared at her, smiling, and all eyes in the place focused on her. She gave the bartender a direct deadpan gaze, snorted, then raised her arms and shimmied into her dress.

"Uh, Wanda," Leon said, "the pay here is good. Two bills a week plus twenty-five percent of your tips." He ran his tongue over his lips. "You, you'll be rich by Christmas. You got something special. I'm glad you did this, coming here today. I hope it wasn't an accident that you came to where *I* worked."

"Sweetheart," Wanda said and pinched his nose, "I never try *nothin'* unintentional."

On the back porch at home Wanda settled down with a can of Jax and said to Jadick, "It was easy. They pay better'n I thought they would, too."

Jadick stood in the doorway looking down on Wanda, who was stretched out with her feet in their regular resting spot on the windowsill. She'd shed the spike heels and the summery dress draped down between her spread legs.

"You get any cookies out of it?" he asked. "You get any kind of kick stripping off in front of them guys?"

"Oh, man," Wanda said, "lemonade has got more kick to it than bare-assin' it in front of men like them. I mean, if they knew what to do with a naked gal they wouldn't be out there studyin' up on it, would they?"

"You wouldn't think so," Jadick said. "The layout sounds a little hairy but I think we can handle it."

"We've got to sober up your desperadoes," Wanda said. "They been in the cold shower for ten minutes but that ain't going to get them sober." She stood up and started wearily toward the kitchen. "I'll have to heat up the fryer and feed them something."

"That's awful sweet and wifey of you," Jadick said.

Wanda laid one of her flattest looks on him, then ducked under his arm across the doorway.

"I'm in this thing way too deep not to want it to work," she said.

Thirty minutes later the deep-fat fryer was sizzling and Wanda was turning out a giant platter of golden brown home fries.

"There ain't no meat in the house," she said as she watched the fryer steam, and heard the grease pop and hiss. "Which is a pity 'cause I fry chicken so all-around special even you boys might take up with women."

Dean and Cecil sat at the table, having already shoveled away the first small portion of fries. Their plates were streaked with fat and ketchup, and Cecil used his finger to etch a heart in the congealing grease.

"I *been* married," Dean said, still shaky on his chair. "To a woman, I mean."

"What was she like?" Wanda asked.

"Pretty tight for a gal with three kids. What kind of question is that, though?"

"A dumb one," Wanda said, and meant it.

There was a pot of coffee on the table and Jadick made his cohorts partake heavily of it. He sat like an overseer, directing the fellas to eat more of them taters, drink more java, think more clearly and listen up.

"I wonder if you guys have been hearing me," he said.

"We heard," Cecil said. Even his voice was puny and pale as his skin and hair. "We done rougher things."

"The timing has to be just right," Jadick said forcefully. "A stickup man has got to have timing—like a comedian. Robbery and comedy have a lot in common, 'cause if the punch line is slow, then the joke is really on the teller. Rob someplace with your timing off a heartbeat this way or that and it ain't gonna be *too* damn much fun. You guys hear me?"

"We ain't in this for the fun," Dean said. His lips pulled back and his greenish teeth went on display. He laughed and Cecil matched his giddy wheeze with his own high-pitched screech. "We're in it for the glory, ain't we Cecil?"

The fun buddies went AWOL, lost to some secret mirth, and Jadick stood up and went onto the porch.

Wanda poured the last basket of fries onto the platter, then set the platter on the table in front of the still cackling men.

She went to the porch herself, then, and found Jadick sitting on the chair arm, bent forward in the thinker's pose, with his chin resting on his fist.

"What you thinkin'?" she asked.

"A deep thought, pun-kin."

"Oh, yeah? Which one?"

"The one where I like to imagine the sun rising tomorrow and me still bein' alive to see it."

"Oh," Wanda said, and waved her hand at him with disappointment, "*that* one."

11

In the year of 1753, way downriver in the Crescent City, the Marquis de Vaudreuil was the appointed governor, and under the stewardship of this grand and elegant European one of the first truly successful ongoing criminal enterprises in North America flourished. The marquis's soldiers shook down the *cantine* owners along the docks, taking wine and rum as payment, and they patronized the bordellos where "correction girls," who'd been imported by the romantic governor, charmed these law-and-order types gratis, and with enthusiasm. There was tremendous eighteenth-century skim from all the city's affairs. The soldiers arrested or murdered any of the citizenry who defied them or insisted upon their right to two-step to the screech of a different fiddler, and soon this noble corruption spread and several of the soldiers turned sullen with success and began to hold out on the Grand Mamou himself.

Marcel Frechette, a Gallic entrepreneurial sort from near Calais, had enlisted under de Vaudreuil partly because his sales techniques had become too celebrated in the old hometown, but mainly because he liked the soldiers' hats. In the New World he very quickly found that being the law bore fruit that no mere gimmick could ever bear, and he shook down the pimps and the prostitutes, grogshop owners, and aristocrats with secret pastimes they preferred to keep that way. Frechette's zeal in his pursuit of other people's do-re-mi soon led him to decide that the governor's piece of the ice was too large, for wasn't he the one who parried the blades and bludgeons of those who were slow to pay? The Marquis de Vaudreuil, famed for the haute couture he and his wife flaunted on all the gay occasions, had standards to uphold, so he sent a squad of good, loyal policemen to bring him this insolent Frechette, an alligator, and a bamboo cage.

In an upstairs rumpus room on Rampart Street, Frechette learned of the shift in the marquis's sentiments from a love-struck fourteen-year-old whore, and set off quickly toward the river where a demonstration of fine Spanish cutlery was required to secure a canoe for himself and the girl, who went by the name of Nathalie. They scurried upriver from the Gulf, paddling close to the bank day after day after day, until he saw a few modest mounds rising from the general soak. He called the hills Les Petites Côtes and appointed himself seigneur of the mounds, the marsh, and that stretch of the river. With the aid of the robust and uncomplaining Nathalie, Frechette hacked out space for a house and built a home overlooking the swamp.

He entered the fur trade and fucked the Indians via pelt prices that fluctuated downwardly from drink to drink, and soon he prospered. Alas, he did so well that other rugged entrepreneurial types paddled north and muscled in on the fur biz, and Frechette's aromatic past caught up to him in the person of one Pierre Blaise whose downriver brother had been slashed to death over a canoe. Blaise's harsh comments forced a duel on the mound that was to become known as Frechette Park, in commemoration of the better shot.

Marcel and Nathalie spawned a slew of children who would make river travel dangerous for another generation, and the old man lived on and on, and a town named St. Bruno wobbled up around him, and in the last summer of his four-score-and-two life, he saw the old Frenchtown streets paved with the red cobblestones that still stood up to modern traffic.

Detective Rene Shade now buzzed over those thumpety-thumpety brick streets, riding on the passenger side of Shuggie Zeck's showboat El Dorado. Shade slumped in the seat and lay back, his eyes steady, staring out the window. The car sped past the cracked sidewalk, loitering corners of Frogtown, where the anarcho-capitalism of the street daffies was theorized, praised, and practiced. Misery was the lectern, and a gin rage the motivation, for meandering, harshly phrased harangues, and Shade and Shuggie had come up that way, hearing them all, believing most. In the thick summer offensive of heat and humidity, the cop and the hood rode in air-conditioned plushery through the worn, slick streets where the T-shirted sweaty backbones of democracy staggered about, drunk with despair or loaded on imported hope, game for any free enterprise that resulted in cash.

"How far to Gumbo?" Shade asked.

"Twenty minutes," Shuggie answered. "Unless the water's up."

They rode the blacktop north, parallel to the river. The land was flat and sogged with swamp and overgrown with indistinct greenery. The road slithered through the backwater country in a series of curves and loops necessitated by the need for solid ground. On either side of the paved surface the sloughs were coated completely by lily pads that gently heaved on the water like breathing ribs.

"Shuggie, you figure we'll have to butch down on this tush hog Gillette?"

"If we find him." Shuggie pointed to the glove box. "There's a pint of cherry vodka in there—hand it to me, uh?"

Shade opened the glove box.

"Cherry vodka? You still drink cherry vodka?"

"What's wrong with that?"

"I haven't had any for a long time, that's all." Shade handed the bottle to Shuggie. "I think it was when the Twist was new, the last time I drank cherry vodka."

"I'm proud of how you've grown all up, Rene," Shuggie said as he unscrewed the top. He took a gentlemanly swallow. "I happen to have a sweet tooth, and I *ain't* apologizin' for it."

As the car whipped down the back road Shade thought of his brother, Francois, who was an assistant D.A., and wondered if li'l bro Frankie could bail his ass out if this thing went Byzantine on him. And somehow the thought of Francois rewound the years and Shade was remembering a time when he, Francois, and this very same Shuggie had set off on an adventure together. It had been the fourteenth birthday of big brother Tip, and Shade, nine years old and earnest, wanted to find a present suitable for presentation to an idol. For this was in the time when Tip, with his already deep chest and huge arms, his street-stompin' rep that was even then spreading beyond Frogtown, was his hero. He sort of worshiped his own brother because didn't grown men, hardasses themselves in some cases, nod to Tip and give him wide berth? And Tip, with his variety of sucker punches and his horseshoe-tapped army boots, had the back-alley swagger that inspired young Rene and Francois and Rene's good pal Shuggie.

They would watch Tip as he stood on the roof of the row house putting pigeons, his odd choice of a hobby, through tumbles and tumults and a whole vaudeville of tricks. And on this birthdate it had been Shuggie who'd solved the gift mystery for Rene by saying, "He loves them birds on the roof—I know where we can get some more."

Young Isaac "Shuggie" Zeck led the expedition to Second Street and St. Peter's Cathedral, where he leaned against the bricks that had been faded by several generations of weather, and said, "Let's climb." He latched onto a drainpipe, then with blubbery bravado mountaineered up the cathedral wall until he came to a section where brick ornamentations jutted out, making for excellent handholds.

Once the trio was on the roof, in between the steep peaks, they began walking in the rain gutters looking for nests and trying not to stare down to the sidewalks where they would certainly splatter if they fell. Flocks of pigeons winged about overhead, scudding like cannon-shot clouds, while the boys kicked through nests, coming up with only two possibly rotten eggs. They put the eggs in a brown lunch sack, then sat at an angle on the steep peak, below the huge cross, their sneakered feet braced in the gutter. They were forlorn, for two paltry eggs were clearly insufficient gift for an idol.

Soon Shuggie began to swivel his head, staring here and there, down, and then up, where he spied a veritable thatch of nests on the flat space beneath the cross. He brought this to everyone's attention. "I don't think so," Rene said. He held the sack with its miserable offering, then studied the path to the cross, the climb up the steeply angled slippery roof, and said, "No way." Li'l brother Francois concurred mutely, merely running his bug eyes to the nests and shaking his head.

"Aw, give me the sack," Shuggie said, snatching it from Rene. Then he set off. He went up fast and low, his fat heinie bouncing with each step of his short legs, the laces of his high-tops flopping loose to the sides of his feet. Rene watched open-mouthed, his mind envisioning the one misstep on the steep incline and Shuggie sliding down, beyond control, whooshing off the roof in a deadly plummet, wafting to the sidewalk like something spit from the steeple. But, no, young Shuggie humped up the daunting path with a positively inspiring disdain for consequences. He breathed hard and his cheeks flushed, but he reached the nests and pillaged the eggs. For his descent he sat on the tiles with the sack at his side, inching down, but then, his feet raised, he flopped onto his back, and accelerated. There was hardly time to react. Rene and Francois stood motionless, shocked, expecting to be clipped by the tumbling Shuggie and dashed below.

Shuggie put his feet down like brakes and stopped on a dime. "I wish you could see the looks on your faces," he said, laughing. He opened the sack and checked on the looted eggs. "I didn't break a one. Let's go."

Big Tip, the birthday boy, was run down on Voltaire Street, outside The Chalk and Stroke, where he occupied an exalted spot against the wall, surrounded by lesser badasses. Rene approached him with the sack and held it to him. "Happy birthday from us guys," he said, gesturing at Francois and Shuggie. Tip stayed against the wall but held out his hand and accepted the gift. When he opened the sack, Rudy Regot and Harky Gifford and Lou Pelitier rubbernecked over his shoulder. Tip spit, then closed the sack and twisted the top. "Them's mongrel eggs," he said, then whipped his arm like he was snapping locker-room butt with a towel and smashed the sack against the bricks. He then lifted the sack by the bottom, turned it over, and drained the mongrel muck to the hot sidewalk, where it made a stain that lasted for months.

When Shuggie wheeled the El Dorado off of the hard road and onto the dirt, the jolt pulled Shade out of the past.

He looked at Shuggie and asked, "Do we have a plan, Shug?"

Shuggie wagged his head but kept his eyes on the narrow dirt road.

"We'll try the classic approach, man," he said. "Hustle in through the door with our guns out and see what runs."

"That's asking for disaster," Shade said.

Shuggie groaned. He raised the cherry vodka and treated himself to a nice long drink.

"Man, send out for some balls," he said harshly. "If these are the tush hogs we're lookin' for you're goin' to be *glad* you got that gun out."

"And if it's *not* them?"

"Uh, well, we'll make a strong first impression on 'em." Shuggie grinned. "That's one of the keys to a new relationship, you know—the first impression."

A few minutes later they began to pass houses built on stilts, raised aloft in recognition of the region's regular floods. Shuggie slowed before a yellow house made of thin, warping wood planks. There was a dirt yard worn down smooth as a defendant's bench. The windows were *sans* screens, allowing open-range rights to an occasional bat and all manner of smaller, winging specks of misery.

"His truck ain't here," Shuggie said. He leaned on the gas. "We'll go on down the road to The Boylin' Kettle. That's the local watering hole."

The bar looked just like any other house except for the gravel parking lot and a handpainted sign nailed to a loblolly pine that read THE BOYLIN' KETTLE.

Shuggie parked behind a pea-green truck, raised high on swamp tires. There was a sticker on the truck's rear bumper that said Coonasses Do It in the Dark.

"That's his pickup," Shuggie said. "We got him."

Shade checked his pistol, knowing that there were no dull followers of the law out here, and that the local populace was mightily leavened by 'backy-chawin' muskrat bashers, whose business lives were attuned to the illegal games markets, St. Brunians' vacation schedules, and the low-flying international aviators who patronized their modest backwoods landing strips.

"If there's more than six coonasses in there," Shade said, "we should give it a skip and catch him alone. I don't have any jurisdiction out here."

"For Christ sake," Shuggie said disgustedly, "did somebody buy you a subscription to *Redbook* since the old days, or what? Geez!" He reached under the front seat and brought out a well-cared-for sawed-off shotgun. As he slipped shells into the chambers he said, "Man, I bet you can do seventy-seven clever things with tuna now, too, can't you?"

It was at this moment, chided by his old and present rival, that Shade decided it was time to revert to the

101

shitkicker verities. Brazen dash, rough talk, and an ounce or two of mean were clearly required.

"I should be on vacation," he said, "and maybe I am. Trade with me." Shade held his pistol toward Shuggie. "Let me swing that cannon."

Shuggie asked, "Why?"

"Hey, look," Shade said, "you know Gillette when you see him and I don't. That means I've got to take your back, man, and cover your fat ass. There might be a passel of tush hogs in that dive, and I want something *seriously bulldog* in my hands when I come through that door. Now give me that double-barrel."

A slow, tense smile moved onto Shuggie's face.

"I hear you, man," he said, and they made the trade.

By the time they'd stepped out of the car, Shade had adopted a shrewd personification of those ancient shitkicker verities, and went toward the door with his shoulders back, chin up, eyes straight, in the long striding saunter of the rough n' ready.

"Now I recognize you," Shuggie said, walking beside Shade with the same stride and posture. "Now you look like the Rene Shade I used to know. Man, it's good to see you again."

The sun was behind the high branches of the tall timeless trees, giving a nice shadowiness to their movements as they went up the three slabwood steps to The Boylin' Kettle.

"Come on," Shade said. "We'll cut through these tush hogs like a rake through shit."

Bobby Gillette looked like a boy soprano who'd fallen in with the wrong crowd for twenty years or so and liked it. He had a frothy wave of sandy hair breaking down his forehead, and big soulful brown eyes and thin lips. When lying down he would've been perfect for measuring off two yards of cotton muslin, but when the bad-news duo came in the door he was sitting at a round table in the center of the room, nursing a Michelob, reading a copy of *Outdoor Life*.

"P'pere," he said to the old man behind the bar. Then he recognized Shuggie and added, "Oh, pas de merde."

Shuggie cocked the police .38 in his hand and held it barrel-up, palm toward Gillette.

"Bonjer, Bobby," he said, and stood over his target. "Some fool bizness went down in town, there, Bobby. Are you the guy who done it?"

Gillette turned a page of the magazine, aping nonchalance, and said, "I don't know, I might be. I'm a nasty motherfucker on a regular basis."

Shade stood just inside the door, his hand on the shotgun, the shotgun resting on the plywood surface of the bar. He looked at the old man behind the rail and the trio of drinking men in sweat-soaked shirts at the other end of the bar.

"Keep your hands where I can see them, Jethro," he said to the bartender. "That goes for you fellas, too. I filed the trigger on this sucker, so it'll spring off if I breathe too deep. I thought y'all should know that."

In the center of the room Shuggie was gently tracing a part in Gillette's hair with the pistol barrel, gentling the blue steel along the top of his skull.

"Whoever done it killed a man," he said sweetly.

"C'est triste," Gillette responded.

"Speak English, coonass," Shade barked. Shade was half-and-half, Franco-Irish American, but at the moment it was the Irish side he identified with. He spoke no more

French than "bonjour," "merci," and a few other phrases, and thought the whole business of bilingualism was a trendy gimmick. "Or I'll give you something to 'c'est triste' about."

"Better listen to him," Shuggie said. "My man over there'll chew your face off and shit it in your mommy's roux, you mess with him."

Gillette sat up, stiffly erect, his hands on the table. He said, "I feel another phony burglary beef comin' on, Zeck."

"Worse," Shuggie said. "You know what worse adds up to, don'tcha, Bob? Huh? Worse means you could be chunked out and baitin' a meaty trotline by dawn."

Still stiff, as the police .38 rested on his head, Gillette said, "Man, I didn't do it, whatever it was. That other thing, back you know when, I did do. I did that. But I ain't done nothin' in St. Bruno since."

The Boylin' Kettle was basically the living room of a three-room house, with two refrigerators for coolers and a flat piece of plywood laid over three flour hogsheads to make a bar. The walls were the same color of green that would have set in on yesterday's fatally wounded, and there were half a dozen mounted fish on them gathering dust. A large upright radio quietly played some Belton Richard chanky-chank.

"Come on this side of the rail, Jethro," Shade said to the bartender, who was an impressively moustached man, pushing seventy and slowly wasting. When he had joined the three patrons, Shade said, "Get on the floor, hands behind your heads." The quartet of bossed boozers acted as if they might raise an objection to these proceedings, but this notion was promptly overruled when Shade bandied the shotgun about. "Facedown," he said, and they silently obeyed.

Now in control of things, Shade scanned the room and the bar and noted that every one of these swamp rats had been drinking bottles of Michelob and that there were cases of the same stacked between the refrigerators. Instantly curious about this astonishing market penetration by such a Yupscale brew, Shade asked, "Y'all hijack a beer truck lately, or what?"

The answer came from Gillette, who said, "If we did it wasn't in St. Bruno, man."

This brought Shade to Shuggie's side, and he nodded at his partner. "Ask him some pointed questions, Shug."

"Were you in town yesterday, man-sewer?" Shuggie asked.

Gillette was doing a fair imitation of stone, and only his lips moved when he answered, "No, man. I been here, swillin' the Michelob, all this time."

Shuggie grabbed Gillette by the collar, then booted the chair from beneath him and pulled on the collar simultaneously, toppling him to the floor, jamming his face to the wood.

"Lie!" Shuggie said loudly, then fired a shot next to Gillette's head, raising an energetic billow of dust. "A little birdie seen you, Bob. Little birdies don't lie. They ain't got it in 'em. You do."

Gillette's lips had split when his face met the floor and an elastic blood drool stretched down his chin and back to the ground. He shook his head groggily, whipping the bloodstrand like a lariat, and flinched when Shuggie blasted another round.

Shade turned to the cowering quartet and said, "I could

grind all of y'all with one twitch, so stay down." Then he leaned to Gillette. "See here, sport," he said, "I don't want to have to watch you stain this nice wood floor from wall to wall. Y'all got yourselves a sweet drinkin' spot here and it'd be a shame if in years to come ol' P'pere over there had to bore himself and every new patron with a long sad explanation for your stains, man. So answer up and I'll hold Shuggie off you."

With bright, glassy eyes Gillette turned and faced Shade, one hand on the floor, the other swatting at the elastic bloodstrand, strumming it like the E-string on an upright bass.

"You changed parts," he said. "First he was Jeff and you was Mutt. Now he's comin' on Mutt and you get to be Jeff." He laughed. "I seen this good man—bad man thing before."

Shade stood tall and straight and kicked Gillette in the stomach. He then lifted his leg with his knee held out before him and jabbed his toes into Gillette's chest.

"It's Mutt and Mutt time, coonass!" he said.

Shuggie put some Italian shoe leather to work on Gillette's back, and Shade flicked his toes into his belly, keeping up the thumping reel until the tush hog tuckered out and collapsed on his side, moaning bluesily and sucking for sweet air.

Shade took a glance at the four prone bystanders and said, "Y'all be still and mind your own business." He then bent forward and leaned over Gillette. "We ain't near tired yet, so you best tell us something secret that we really, *really*, want to know."

"Aw, man, I heard, I heard about it," Gillette said. He held his hands to his belly and curled his legs up to block any further dance steps to his guts. His head was sideways to the floor and crimson slobber was smeared on his cheeks. "There ain't no problem with my left tit," he said and tapped some fingers to his heart. "My left tit ain't got no dog in it, but I ain't doin' no more time for another crime I never even got the fun of pullin'."

The radio crackled with D. L. Menard droning "The Back Door," and a long beam of light from the sliding sun came through the southwest window and glinted off the cases of beer stacked between the refrigerators. The four men who stood a good chance of becoming possibly innocent victims, kept their hands on their heads and their noses to the wood and their opinions to themselves.

"I heard today what happen last night," Gillette said, "but day last I seen a man I know who whisper to me that a man he knows is in town who shouldn't be." Accompanied by a couple of convincing grimaces, Gillette sat up. "Oh, you town dudes—I don't fuck with you. Believe you that. This man who is in the town was not so long ago in the federal place, eh? Braxton. What I am told is that he run with a prison clique calls itself The Wing."

"Where'd your friend see this fella?" Shuggie asked.

"Buyin' gin and lime juice at Langlois' Liquor, there. In town." Gillette spit a heavy globule of blood and saliva that spun through the air and hit the wall a good ten feet away. "He had a partner, and this clique is s'posed to be dangerous more than a little."

"Are they the fellas we're lookin' for?" Shade asked.

"That I don't know for positive," Gillette said. "But they was in town, here, and they don't belong here."

Shade and Shuggie exchanged glances and with barely perceptible nods they agreed to several things: that

Gillette's info was interesting; that he was probably not involved; and that they wouldn't be capping anyone in The Boylin' Kettle.

"You hear a name on the out-of-town dude?" Shuggie asked.

"Well," Gillette said, "it was Cecil something." Gillette kept his face down and used his fingers to swab at the blood drools on his face. "Don't hit me no more, eh? Could be I don't know nothin' else."

"Okay," Shade said and walked over to the prone men. He stood near their feet with the shotgun loosely aimed at their backs. "Cough up all y'all's car keys, hear me? One at a time you're going to reach into your pockets and fish out your keys and toss 'em on the floor." He nudged the man on the left with a foot to the ankle. "Startin' with you, sport."

While Shade did his forcible valet thing, Shuggie lifted the chair from the floor and said, "Have a seat, Bobby. You got lucky last time and I don't believe you'd be stretchin' your good gris-gris this tight again." Gillette sat in the chair and slumped forward onto the table, a small afterflow of the crimson juice flecking the magazine he'd been reading peaceably when the day had so suddenly gone awful on him. Shuggie said, "But as you see we *can* find you, and if you bullshitted us we'll be back, *Row-bear*. And prob'ly we'll be all bummed out and hurt, too, hurt that a *confrère* like you would mislead us."

"I didn't, Zeck."

Shade had scooped up all the keys except Gillette's but the stomped man put his on the table without being asked. Shade stuffed all the keys into his pants pockets.

"I'll drop 'em in the middle of the road just before the blacktop starts," he said. He then rapped the sawed-off barrel on the tabletop, drawing Gillette's eyes up to his. "Now don't even think about loadin' up and comin' into Frogtown lookin' for us, man, 'cause your luck might run out and you'd *find* us."

With that the inquiring duo backed to the door where Shuggie paused and said, "This was only bizness, guys— no hard feelings, all right?"

From The Boylin' Kettle to the paved road Shuggie's El Dorado whipped up a dust trail and slalomed through the curves. He hit the brakes when he sighted blacktop and Shade rolled his window down and tossed a jangling variety of car keys into the dust. Then Shuggie tromped on the gas and swung off the soft dirt and onto the hard road, and roared toward town, displaying a road-hog outlook by taking the middle of the blacktop for his lane.

"We done good," he said to Shade. "You ever heard of this thing, this gang—The Wing?"

"No," Shade said. The shotgun rested on the floorboard between his feet just in case the coonasses knew some secret shortcut and lay in wait, fomenting an unpleasant reunion. "There's dozens of those prison cliques, Shuggie. The Wing I don't know."

"We'll ask around," Shuggie said. The pint of cherry vodka was on the front seat and he lifted it. "I gotta say, that was purty damn slick," he said, laughing. When he saw that Shade was unsmiling, he added, "Cut the long-face phony thing, Rene—I know you. You were wired and primed back there, man. You had your rumble hat on and don't bother tellin' me I'm wrong."

Shade did laugh and stretched his legs and leaned back in the soft plush seat.

"That business points up a po-lease man's constant dilemma," he said, laughing with a combination of relief and exhilaration. "Anybody who's ever done any crime knows that it *can be* a fuckin' hoot."

"We both been knowin' *that* for a while," Shuggie said. "Sometimes I recall things we done years ago, Rene, when we was a team and hungry." He slowly shook his curly-haired head. "I never feel ashamed *at all*."

"I believe you," Shade said, mirthlessly, staring out the window. "But sometimes *I* do."

The day had zipped by Shade, lulled as he was by fatigue, propelled as he was by speed, and as the sun dove behind the tall marsh trees and the shadows loomed long and deep across the road he traveled down, he retreated once again into memory. It was the day of Shuggie's wedding to his astutely chosen bride, and St. Peter's was SRO, for the Langlois clan was large and widespread with kin in every quarter of the city, and the Zecks had a few friends, too. Shade had been put into a tux as a grooms-man, along with Rudy Regot and Kenny Poncelet, while Shuggie's older brother Bill had been best man. That had been the last time Shade and Shuggie had been close, and after Father Marty Perroni had legally linked Zeck to Langlois, they'd all gone to a reception in The Huey Long Room of The St. Bruno Hotel and everyone was there: Auguste Beaurain sipped a glass of Champale while his then chief lieutenant, Denis Figg, who was soon to disappear during the unpleasantness with the upriver dagos, hovered nearby; and old Mayor Atlee Yarborough had acted real "just folks" and goosed a teen-aged bridesmaid, repeatedly, to her consternation and the voters' joy; and Shade and Shuggie and Kenny Poncelet who died at Quong Tri and Tip and How Blanchette and the whole cast from the melodrama of childhood, had put Cold

Duck away until the cows came home and the groom had required pouring into a rented black sedan, and Hedda had driven off toward a supposed honeymoon at Panama Beach.

Now, straddling that little white line toward Frogtown, Shade said, "You ever tell your father-in-law about all the times we ripped him off?"

"No, I never did."

"You don't think he'd find it enlightening? Or funny?"

Shuggie grunted, smiling.

"Actually, Daddy Langlois has bitched about the neighborhood thieves plenty, but I never say anything, although Hedda knows. I thought it might seem endearing, you know, like an old movie, so I told her one time." Shuggie took a sip of cherry vodka. "She's been holdin' it over my head ever since."

"I haven't seen Hedda to talk to in years," Shade said. "She always says, 'Hi, Rene,' and keeps going when I run into her."

"What'd you expect? You're a cop. Nobody likes cops. Cops cause nothin' but trouble."

"Yeah, yeah, I know," Shade said lightly, "but how *is* Hedda?"

"Fine, fine. She still likes to grease up and sit on the hog of an evenin', but we been married forever it seems like, man."

"Since what? Nineteen?"

"Yeah. Since the fun old days."

Soon they were within the city limits, back in Frogtown, rumbling over those thumpety-thumpety bricks that had been laid down so long ago, and Shuggie said, "Someday you're goin' to explain to me why you're a cop. Why that is, is because I can still remember when you and me plotted and plotted in our kid way, you know, dreamin' of growin' up and shovin' Mr. B. and Steve Roque and all those bossmen out of the boat and into the river."

"And we'd be top dogs," Shade said. "I remember when we dreamed that trash."

There were a couple of inches of sweetish booze left in the bottle and Shuggie held it in his hand.

"We figured we could outsmart 'em and take 'em off once we got seasoned."

Shade nodded and said, "I know we did."

After a swallow Shuggie held the bottle toward Shade.

"We still could," he said.

Smiling tightly, Shade looked out the window, then turned to Shuggie, who watched him intently. Then both men laughed and Shade wordlessly took the bottle, raised it and drained it, dropping the dead soldier to the floorboard where it slid with a ding into the sawed-off shotgun, and laid there.

12

Mother Nature was laying down some Law out there in the bayou night, and as befits the order of things, large feathered creatures dove off high branches, swooped low and stuck talons in smaller furry meals, and bandit-eyed coons came stealthily out of hollow logs and glommed finned, scaly chow from the still, brackish shallows, while all those things that slither waited, coiled, for the passing appearance of any prey absentminded, and where the bayou waters butted against land and a screened porch overlooked the boggy stage for these food-chain theatricals, Emil Jadick sat on the arm of the couch and wrapped up a lecture that had been real Type A in tone and content.

He said, "And if either of you fucks up because you ain't been listenin' to me, I'll take you off the calendar myself, understood?"

Dean Pugh and Cecil Byrne sat on the couch, forearms on knees, heads down, sullenly nodding.

"We listened, Jadick," Dean said, raising his head. "And we been here before, Mr. Boss Hoss."

"You got caught before," Jadick said. "I'd like to avoid that—so don't fuck up."

Pugh and Byrne were both essentially state-raised social problems, government-parented misfits. They'd lived the institutional life in different places, Dean from age eight in Maryland, and Cecil from age four in Florida, and met at what somehow seemed to them to be the bosom of their family—the federal pen. Both men moved with that odd, fearful underdog gait, jerking around like disoriented lizards, gawkily uncoordinated, stoically confused.

"We're gonna back you up all the way," Dean said. "'Cause what is it that *always* flies above the shit?"

"The Wing," Jadick said in unison with Cecil. "The Wing soars above it."

"There it is, brother."

Wanda was in the kitchen where she'd listened to Jadick's pep talk while doing the dishes. She began to dry the plates and silverware with a towel, and Jadick walked up behind her and cupped her breasts.

"Do all men do that?" she asked, not missing a stroke.

"Do what?"

"Get the hots for women in the kitchen." She shook her head quizzically. "Every man I ever been around gets all touchy-feely when I do dishes or cook."

Jadick backed away and sat at the table.

"I'd have to think about that," he said.

Wanda put the dried dishes in the cupboard, then got herself a cup of coffee. She leaned against the counter, holding the cup.

"Is your gang up to it?" she asked in a low voice.

Jadick shrugged.

"They're givin' the right answers," he said.

"Oh, man," Wanda said, "I've heard beer farts that made more sense than them two."

"Shut the fuck up," Jadick said. He studied her closely, eyes narrowed. "Don't plant bad seeds, pun-kin. Don't plant no bad seeds in me when you *know* we got a job tonight."

She blew on her coffee and looked at him over the rim of the cup.

"I'm just concerned," she said. "That's all."

"Now, look," Jadick said, "the upshot is . . ."

". . . Oh, I dread that," Wanda said, turning away.

"Dread what?"

"The upshot. Man, I dread that motherfucker."

At this moment Dean and Cecil came in from the porch, grinning and bouncing with criminal vim. Dean put an arm around Cecil's shoulders, face beaming, and said, "You know, I *like* my life. Really, I do. Lots of people would say it's a shitty kind of life, but I don't. I like my life, you know. Things happen in it. I don't see how as that should be considered shitty. Everybody has things that happen in their life, but I *like* the things that happen in mine."

Jadick slowly swiveled his gaze from Dean to Wanda, then he pointed an admonishing finger at her.

"You got anything to say to that, pun-kin?"

Wanda leaned back on the counter and raised her eyes to the naked bulb on the ceiling, shuddering though smiling, and said, "Well, now, ain't *everything* just *beau*tiful, in its own way."

When Shade came trudging up the dark sidewalk and in through Nicole Webb's front door, Sleepy LaBeef was cranked up on the speakers, singing a wry and lively country boogie about the path he'd taken to The Wayside Lounge. Nicole was in the kitchen leaning over a pan of boiling water, turning crawdads into food. She wore a long cotton country dress that was festooned with flowery things that had been paled by repeated washings. Her feet were bare, her long hair was a dark unbrushed bramble, and she wore her black-framed reading glasses. Her back was turned to Shade, her eyes were focused on the reddening mud lobsters. She said, "I heard you come in, Rene, so don't bother sneakin' up behind me and grabbin' my butt."

"I don't like sneaks either," he said. He walked over and reached below the hem of her dress and raised his hand to the split where it lingered. "Sorry about today," he said into her ear. "A cop was shot."

"I heard," she said. She put stove gloves on her hands and raised the bucket of crawdads. "Now watch out," she said, "they're done."

Shade opened the refrigerator and saw a stock of long-necked Texas beer, and selected one, then sat at the kitchen table. As was the case with most flat spaces in Nic's house, the tabletop had several books laid open to the spine on it. *The Women at Point Sur, A Moveable Feast*, something about Vermeer and two novels by Shirley Ann Grau were spread out for handy reading while cooking.

"What're you making?"

"Crawdads, yellow rice and sliced tomatoes—any complaints?"

"No."

"That's damned good news if you feel like eatin'. 'Cause this is it."

From birth to the age of eighteen, Nicole had called Port Lavaca, Texas, home. She'd been raised up smelling the salt air of the Gulf and it seemed even now that her gaze was naturally trained on the distant horizon. During her final year in high school, she'd busted her hump both before and after class peeling shrimp at the dock, saving every penny for postgraduation flight. It was Italy that she fled to, along with Sandy Colter, her lifelong best friend. But after eight weeks Sandy said she had some problems with the water, the men, the women, the dogs, the motor scooters, and "all the fucking garlic," and went home. Nicole stayed on alone and tried to go native in Trieste. Months later on a rambling excursion to Greece, she took the ferry from Brindisi to Patras and overheard two long-hairs speaking with Texas accents and suddenly the sky opened and she was hunkered down with them beneath a rainslicker, sucking on a bottle of ouzo while puddles developed around their feet.

The more charming Texan was named Keith Goodis and he claimed he was a stock-car driver in his mind, and would soon be so in fact. Two weeks later she was back in Trieste by herself, and behind a sense of heightened loneliness she began to find the Old World to be crotchety rather than charming, and flew home.

In Port Lavaca she stuffed the necessities of her life into an army surplus duffel bag and thumbed to Austin, where she presented herself on Keith Goodis's doorstep, and was welcomed. For the next three years, while Keith tried to prove himself on the oval dirt tracks of the South, she went to the university with the vague notion of turning herself into something decent, like an English teacher. But as time went by a certain sour melody sound-tracked her days, for good ol' Keith had fallen into the trap of loving a life he had small talent for, and after seventeen straight Sunday finishes out of the money he blamed her and domesticity for leeching from his soul the wildness required by his career, and she responded with an unkind comment or two concerning hand-eye coordination and pudding for brains.

The next day she deep-sixed education and called her old friend Sandy, who told her she'd finally found her true self in St. Bruno, where she lived with her friend Kathleen and had a neat little business renovating and refurbishing old houses. Come on over, she said, and Nicole did. Nic worked with Sandy and Kathleen until Kathleen began to resent her for having known Sandy since infancy, and she went hungry for a while, then took a job at Maggie's Keyhole. She was now twenty-eight and at home in Frogtown and at ease with Shade, but there was still something quietly unsettled about her that made it seem she was only marking time.

As Nicole set the bowl of crawdads along with rice and tomatoes on the table, Shade said, "What's with the fridge full of Texas longnecks?"

"Oh, now and then I can't help gettin' sentimental for some Lone Star."

"Uh-huh," Shade said. He filled his plate with a glob of everything, then belted back some brew. He was pulling the tail off a crawdad when he said, "I'll bet Lone Star was ol' *Keith*'s favorite pabulum, *wudn't* it?"

"Don't do that," she said. "Please—it knocks you down in my eyes."

"All right," he said. "I hear you." Ever since she'd made the mistake of telling him the details of her previous major fling he'd needled her about it, usually by implying that she'd been love-suckered by a crybaby. "The mud lobster is done *just right*," he said.

"Thank you."

While dinner was eaten Nicole told Shade that How Blanchette was looking for him and would be at Ma Blanqui's early, early in the morning. She then segued into a pretty passionate explanation of Robinson Jeffers's "inhumanism" and he nodded cunningly as her whole theory whooshed right past him. During a lull in her explication he explained to her that he was flattened out from postspeed-sag and fatigue and that he might have to get back on the street in a few hours. What he needed was to relax.

After the meal Nicole put a stack of Nanci Griffith albums on the stereo, filled a yellow salad bowl with ice, then stuck in bottles of beer. She went into the bedroom and came back with two joints and a lighter and said, "Come on into the backyard, Rene, and smooth your ragged self out."

Shade followed her outside and they sat on the concrete blocks that served as back steps. The yard was not much larger than a regulation billiard table, squared off by the neighbors' fences, screened in somewhat by the honeysuckle that grew on those chicken wires. Several cottonwood trees rose up and spread out, partially blocking the light cast by a half-moon on a clear, delta summer night. The previous tenants of this cozy but ramshackle house had had their union blessed by a set of quickly spoiled twins, and a few obsolete toys were trashed along the fencerows, and a pink wading pool with penguins painted on the side sat in the center of the yard.

Shade drank while Nicole smoked, joining her for only

two or three tokes out of a sense of etiquette that was a holdover from his teens. In less time than it takes to drink one cold longneck on a hot night, while Nanci Griffith sang "Spin on a Red Brick Floor," Nicole began to go gypsy beneath the moonglow, dancing exuberantly in a tight circle, spreading her skirt, her rhythmic jostles causing foam to rise from the lips of her bottle and spray about. Soon she came back to the steps and picked up the yellow salad bowl of iced brew, and said, "I feel like a dip in the pool."

The honeysuckle scent flavored the night breeze, and voices laughing at "The Late Movie" carried from nearby houses. Distant hounds howled from pen to pen, relaying the nocturnal edition of the dog news.

Nicole shimmied out of her dress and plopped into the shallow pool.

"Aw, I filled it fresh at dark," she said. "It's cool—come on in. Surf's up."

Shade stood up from the steps and walked over to the pool. He looked around and saw a few upstairs lights on in rooms that had a view of the pool. He drank from his bottle, then looked down to where Nicole reclined, using her hands to cup cool water and splash it onto her chest.

"Rene, don't be bashful," she said, "there's no X-ray eyes around here."

"I'm kinda tired," he said.

"I wanna have fun, Rene."

"Okay," Shade said, and kicked out of his slip-on shoes, then pulled his shirt off and unbuckled his britches, letting them fall, then stepping free. He stood there in his birth suit, drained the beer and tossed the empty into the undergrowth by the fence. "Darlin'," he said as he crouched into the water, "you're fixin' to have yourself *multiple* funs, hear?"

Nicole chuckled and said, "I believe in the deed, honey, not the threat."

A shared beer later, there in the children's wader, beneath the sweet night sky, Shade admitted to feeling chemically limp, and turned to the tongue for amusement. "It must be the French in me," he said, then slithered across the slick pool bottom. He put his hands beneath her hips and raised her pubis to the waterline. He crouched forward, knowing that there were certainly nights, and he'd experienced many of them, when he'd rather be right where he was now, buried in muff, exercising a learned tongue, licking her breathless, his own rocks on hold.

The Wingmen rolled to a stop in the white rock-dust of The Rio, Rio Club parking lot. They'd appropriated a black Trans-Am from the employees' parking lot of an open all-night Kroger's. Cecil sat behind the wheel, the engine running, the headlights doused. The low rumble of the engine heightened the sense of coiled readiness that filled the car. Jadick said, "Masks," and the three of them pulled ski masks on, adjusting the eye slots into satisfactory position. The car rocked while idling and Jadick, from the backseat, said, "Who is it?" and the proper response, "The Wing," came from the front. Jadick then leaned over Dean and opened the door.

"Let's fuck 'em up," he said, and The Wing climbed out, and swooped.

≡ **13** ≡

"This is the part I like," Shuggie Zeck said with a wide smile. He patted Hedda's knee and leaned close to her on the couch, pointing at the TV screen. "Watch this— Red Skelton just has always cracked me up. See?"

Shuggie was in a blue robe, freshly showered and shaved, smelling of Old Spice. He watched the screen with lips parted in a small, constant smile. "I should get back to the club," he said, "but I love this guy."

On the coffee table in front of the couch there were two snifters containing Frangelico over ice. Beside the snifters sat two empty bowls that had a thin coating of ice cream and a few crumbs of peach cobbler growing sticky on the sides.

In the movie Red found himself in Cuba where he was helping a New York society dame get settled into the vine-covered, shutter-slapping spooky mansion that was her haunted inheritance. Skelton's spaz reactions to the living dead who abounded on the estate caused Shuggie to roar and Hedda to smile serenely. In between guffaws Shuggie pulled his socks on, then stood and stepped into a pair of white slacks.

"The hell with it," he said and sat back down. "So I get back to the club a little late— I gotta see the end of this one again." He wiped laughter-tears from the corners of his eyes. "Christ, I loved Red Skelton movies since I don't know when."

"I know since when," Hedda said. She was also in a robe, a red one, and a pink bandeau covered her hair. "Since childhood."

"Yeah," Shuggie said. "I s'pose that's so."

The movie plot had dragged the ever jittery Red Skelton to the house of an old crone who wore silver-dollar earrings and a secretive mien, and Shuggie was watching contentedly, when the phone rang.

On the third ring Shuggie reached to the end table and lifted the receiver. "Yeah," he said. "What? When?" He listened for a few seconds, then said, "Keep the lid on and line up the employees. I'm not happy." He hung up. He turned back to the TV and took a lingering look at the supernatural antics going on, then turned away and stood. He untied the robe and dropped it. He went into the bedroom to finish dressing. As he buttoned his shirt he shouted to his wife, "Hedda, get me that gun that's downstairs behind the furnace!"

"Which gun?"

"The one I filed the serial numbers off!"

Fat Frank Pischelle sat on a barstool in The Rio, Rio holding a bloody towel to a long, vertical gash in his forehead. There were bloodstains on his shirt and on the floor near his feet. Above and behind him there was a huge, splintered hole in the lookout perch on the wall, and smeared, modernist trails of blood streaked down abstractly.

"For the tenth time, Shuggie," Fat Frank said, "they was in the door and pullin' triggers before we even seen 'em. The man with the shotgun, the son of a bitch who bashed my forehead, cut loose on Eddie Barnhill, up there on the wall, *immediately*. He seemed to know right where to shoot." Fat Frank looked up shaking his head. "They wore masks, and like, you know, duck-hunting shirts or whatever. It made them look like they might be efficient or something. They were in charge from the get-go."

Leon Roe came over with a handful of ice and handed it to Fat Frank. Fat Frank said "Thanks" and wrapped the ice in the towel. He leaned forward, gash on the ice, and said, "And like I said, Shug, there ain't been nothin' unusual today. The workmen is all."

"Christ," Shuggie said, slapping a palm against his forehead. "Who is it? Who the fuck are these guys? Hey, they *were* definitely white, right?"

"Yeah," Fat Frank said. "They were white. Man," he said and glanced up at the shotgun perch, "poor Eddie. Poor Eddie."

Shuggie had already spoken to everyone who'd been there who hadn't split, except for Leon Roe. Leon had been making himself useful, getting ice for Frank, a sloe gin fizz for Shuggie, and he'd helped a gambler named Ralph carry Eddie Barnhill's body outside to a pickup truck.

When Shuggie approached, Leon was sitting by the jukebox, his eyes still expanded by the new sights he'd seen, his hands absently rubbing a wet rag on his red-spotted clothes.

Shuggie stood over him. He said, "I talked to Luscious Loni and Panting Patti, kid. They said Sinful Suzie told 'em you'd brought in a new girl today— I guess you forgot that."

"New girl?" Leon said.

Crouching down so that he was eye to eye with Leon, Shuggie said, "So, kid, you ever seen a flick called *Rolling Thunder*?"

"No. No, sir."

"That's too bad. There's some good torture scenes in it. So, kid, tell me about the gal who came in today. You bought her a beer. She's a bricktop gal."

"Bricktop?"

"A redhead."

"Oh."

From his barstool beneath the wall tapestried by gore, Fat Frank said, "Hey, that's right. I forgot about that, Shuggie."

"What's her name, kid," Shuggie said. "This is probably a coincidence, but tell me her name."

"Her name? I think it was, I don't know, Moaning Lisa."

"That's it," Fat Frank said.

"No, no, no," Shuggie said angrily. "Not her fuckin' striptease name—her real name."

"Her real name?" Leon looked down at the tips of his snakeskin boots. "She said it was Wanda."

"Wanda? A bricktop named Wanda?" Shuggie sprang to his feet. "What's the rest of her name?"

"I never knew," Leon said. "I just seen her, you know, at the Kroger's store in Frogtown, there, a few times. She was buying chickens and me, too. I tried to chat her up."

"You know where she lives?"

"No. I guess over by Kroger's."

Shuggie paced up and down the room for a minute or two. He had his hands in his pockets and his head down. Finally he paused.

"This redhead—she about this tall? Big jugs? A few freckles buckshot across her face? She always have this sort of expression on her that says 'Fuck me if you dare'? You know what I mean by that? Is that her?"

Fat Frank lowered the bloody towel from the split in his head, his fingers thoughtfully stretching his salt-and-pepper goatee.

"Oh," he said, "you must know her."

The living room was illuminated by the imageless screen of the television when Shuggie stomped in. The Frangelico bottle was nearly empty and Hedda was stretched out on the couch, facedown, snoring. Shuggie grasped the back of her robe and spun her onto the floor.

As she came awake he stuck two fingers in her mouth, causing her to choke, and said, "Spit it out! Spit it out!"

She slapped at his hands until he removed his fingers from her mouth. Her eyes were bleary but wide and her chins shook.

"What? Shuggie! What?"

"Spit out that bridge I paid eighteen hundred dollars on. I don't want to break it, but I *am* goin' to slap your face, Hedda."

Liquored up and confused as she was, Hedda instinctively began to slide away across the carpet.

"Honey—what?"

"Put your bridge on the table!"

Hedda was trying to do a crab-slide around the coffee table. The TV glow seemed to throw a spotlight on her.

126

"What'd I do? Huh? What'd I do, honey?"

"Take your bridge out," Shuggie said, then began to slap the back of her head. "Take"—slap—"your bridge"—slap—"out."

"Okay, okay okay okay." Hedda hunched forward and slid the bridge out. The bridge included her two front teeth and she set it in one of the empty dessert bowls. "Now what'd I do?"

He leaned over her, hands clasped behind his back, then his left palm came out of the darkness and slapped her across the mouth, and when she pulled away his right hand followed up and bloodied her nose.

"You got a man killed!" he yelled.

"What?" Her face reflected her terror. In fifteen years together Shuggie had never struck her and very rarely raised his voice to her. "I didn't," she said, baffled. "I didn't—what? Kill? Me? No, no, no."

"You been seein' Wanda Bouvier, haven't you? I told you never to talk to her or see her again, but you did, didn't you? I sort of knew you were. I figured you were. I figured you were *despite* what I told you."

Her head was shaking in the negative, blood drizzling down across her lips.

"Who said that? Honey, they're lyin'. Who told you that? I mean . . ."

He backhanded her high on the cheek, and her left eye instantly began ballooning closed.

"It had to be her," Shuggie said. "And that means it had to be *you*. You and your big, floppy-lipped mouth." He collapsed onto the couch, sitting up. "The country club game, that was goin' on for years, so everybody knew about it. Ronnie, too. But this game at Rio, Rio, why, only a few, only just a few knew about *it*." He pointed at his wife's head, his index finger and thumb making a pistol. "You saw her today, didn't you baby? Huh, sugar plum? What was it, lunch, or just a beer? Tell me, sweet lambikins, you meet to eat or just to hoist a couple?"

"Both," Hedda said, dully. The hot urges her husband felt had led to an ominous melt of his facial features, they sagged flat and mad. She was a bloodied heap on the floor. With one eye swollen shut she had to swing her head around to keep him in sight. "You knew all along how I feel about her. She's a good kid, like the li'l sister I never did have. I love her."

"Uh-huh," Shuggie said. "I guess I should keep that in mind. Say, do you remember one time when you and me went to Miami with Eddie Barnhill and his wife—what was her name?"

"It's Emily."

"Yeah," Shuggie said, nodding. "That's it. Emily. Emily's a widow now. As of a couple of hours ago. Eddie's a fuckin' design on the wall at The Rio, Rio and your *li'l* sister who you *love* did it!"

Hedda seemed dumbstruck, mouth open, eyes squinched. Her head shook and she had the look of a woman who had sunk chin-deep in the mire of un-suspected spousal dementia.

"What on earth are you talkin' about? Wanda? Killing people?"

"Yeah," Shuggie said. "She cased the place for a few tush hogs to knock over. My guess is that Ronnie made hisself some new friends in Braxton. Ol' *Ronnie*'s song is sung. Know what I mean? He's a dead man but it might be awhile before his heart gets the news."

Shuggie got up from the couch.

"Now, honey-bunchkins," he said, "I want to know

where she lives these days. I'm gonna *suggest* that you tell me, too, *right now*."

"Oh, Shuggie, she never told me. Don't hit me! She never told me, you see, 'cause she thinks maybe you'd, you know, make trouble for her. 'Cause of what Ronnie done."

Shuggie stood between his wife and the illuminating TV, casting a huge shadow over her, his hands clasped behind his back.

"You seem like you expect me to believe that."

"Oh, I wish you would!"

"Well, you know the truth about wishes, don't you, sweet pea?" he said, and his hands flew.

Later he sat down and stared at his wife. She was curled in the fetal position. A few of her hairs had been pulled out and stuck to his hands. She whimpered and sobbed, her face to the carpet.

"All right," he said, "maybe you *don't* know where she's stayin' anymore. That might make sense. To her it might make sense. But you do have a phone number—right?"

Though this comment was a relief, Hedda suddenly shrieked louder, and slapped her fists against the floor.

"Hush up, honey. I got to think. I got to make a phone call. I got to figure things out." He reached over to the end table and lifted the phone. He dialed a number. "Hello," he said, "Karl? Shuggie. I know, I know, I'm sorry to wake you. Are you awake enough now for me to tell you something? Uh-huh, we did. Yeah. No, we ain't got them yet but I got a lead. Look, Karl, that's what I'm callin' about. I don't think Shade is the man we want on this. Just a sense I have. It's goin' to get nasty. Hear what I'm sayin'? Yeah. Shade might get in the way. You better get me Tommy Mouton. He'll do whatever it takes. Okay. Yeah. And Karl, have him come in a squad car, all right?"

Shuggie hung up the phone. Hedda was still sobbing into the deep shag carpet. There was an inch or two of liqueur left in the Frangelico bottle that they'd shared earlier while watching Red Skelton and the Cubano zombies. He raised the bottle and had a sip.

"Hedda, honey," he said softly. "I'm goin' to tell you what to say, then you're goin' to give Wanda a call. When you give her this call you know what it is you're goin' to do?"

Hedda raised her upper body from the carpet and quickly turned toward her husband, her expression fearful, her face colorized by red smears, lumpy white swells, and blue bruises. She said, "Whatever you tell me, Shug."

14

Wanda Bone Bouvier was being caressed and cuddled on the mottled pink mattress in her bedroom. She was having to endure Emil Jadick's oversqueezing of her ribs and the quick darts of his tongue into her ear. He was talkin' all kinds of trash to her. He was trying to insinuate himself into her future via an interesting cross of sweet syntax and menacing pillow talk. He was giving her the old "I been there and I been here and I been here and there and no-where did I meet a gal who loves me like you do, so strong and tasty and smart, and if you don't be my lovin' woman from now on out I'll *hurt* somebody *bad*."

The candle was lit and flickering in front of the mirror. Wanda wore a red wraparound skirt and one of Ronnie's black T-shirts that stretched down to her knees and said Jack Daniel's Field Tester on it. Emil was curled next to her, still in camouflage. The St. Bruno High Pirates gym bag was at the foot of the bed, open, drooling dollar bills.

"I don't know about hearin' that kind of talk," she said. "I love Ronnie true, Emil. That's a big deal to me."

"You can still love him," Jadick said, his lips skimming

131

along her neck. "You can still love him but second instead of first."

"Uh-huh. You'd be first?"

"Sounds good don't it."

When it came to men Wanda felt like she was basically a highly prized household convenience. Oh, they bird-dogged her sweet and breathy with promises and presents, but only Ronnie stayed sweet after he'd had her awhile.

"I think Ronnie might object to that," she said.

"Not if he was gone."

"What do you mean by that?"

"Well, pun-kin, when Ronnie gets home he could be out here on this river, breathin' free air again, and have himself a fishing accident—couldn't he?"

"I don't think so." Wanda squirmed out of Emil's arms and got off the bed. "I don't believe he could have a fishin' accident—he's strictly a meat-eatin' man."

Wanda started toward the kitchen and Jadick rolled off the bed and followed her.

"You ever seen that much money?" he asked her. "You ever seen the kind of dough The Wing brings in?"

"No, Emil," she said. In the kitchen she opened the cupboards and shoved the yellow-labeled cans of generic soups around, rooting for a snack. "I'm nervous but I'm hungry."

Emil corralled her from behind and bumped his groin to her ass.

"Hungry, huh?" he said. "What are you hungry for?"

She shook free of his arms, went to the fridge. When she opened the door the light flashed in her eyes. She said, "Would a tiny taste of *everything good* be out of the question?"

Though she had her head in the brightly lit fridge he smiled at her. He bobbed his chin. He said, "You weren't actually talkin' to *me* there, were you, pun-kin?"

She closed the fridge door.

"You're right," she said.

"You were talkin' to whatever it is *I* talk to whenever I say, '*Why me?*' Weren't you?"

"I suppose so," she said.

"And you never get no answers do you, Wanda?"

"No," she said. She sat at the table and braced her chin in her hands. "But I think that might be just as well."

When the phone rang Wanda jumped up, startled, and looked at Jadick. After another few rings she shook her head in bafflement, and lifted the receiver.

"Oh, hello," she said.

Jadick went onto the porch. It was beginning to be his favorite spot. He gazed out onto the black bayou and imagined that all the shadows were silhouettes of living things and that all the chirping, buzzing, whirring, splashing sounds were coded human communications used by those silhouettes as they studied him from the bog.

For ten minutes he sat there, hearing Wanda's side of a crazed conversation, imagining himself to be encircled by a band of enemies who mimicked the natural world precisely.

After she hung up she joined him on the couch.

"Who the hell was that callin' you at two forty-five A.M.?"

"Oh, man," Wanda said with a long sigh, "it was my friend Hedda. The one I had lunch with. She's drunk as a lord, man."

"What'd she call you for?"

"I'm her friend. Her husband's Shuggie Zeck, you

133

know? She heard about the Rio, Rio deal and she can't get ahold of him."

"Uh-huh," Jadick said. "She thought he'd be here?"

"No, man, no. Christ, I wouldn't fuck her husband. He's at a big poker game up the road a ways. At the bathhouse at Holiday Beach. There ain't a phone out there and she says he's playin' for the long green, big money." Wanda wagged her head thoughtfully. "She's afraid you all will hit that game, too, and he'll get hurt."

"This place is up the road a ways?"

"A mile. Maybe two."

They sat there silently. The toilet flushed. Bare feet padded in the kitchen. A loud bark wafted over the water. Something splashed. The refrigerator door opened and Cecil said, "Shit, there ain't nothin' to eat."

Jadick said, "Long green, huh?"

"Oh, man, this is too much."

"Big money, huh?"

"Emil? Oh, man, I feel hinky about this. Really I do."

"Put on some coffee," he said. "Quick."

"Coffee?" she said. "Oh, man, you're gonna go for it. Man, you're pushin' it too hard."

"Darlin' girl," Jadick said harshly, "do you know what the Fates are? Huh? Do you?" Jadick squeezed her knee until she writhed. "Well, I'm out to test 'em."

There was one light on when Shade walked into his mother's poolroom. Monique sat on a tall stool near a large red Dr Pepper cooler, vigorously brushing her ankle-length gray hair. In daytime she wore braids circled and pinned up like a crown, but at night it all came down and gave her the appearance of a witch.

"Hey, Ma," Shade said. How Blanchette and Francois

Shade stood leaning against a pool table, rolling the balls against the rails. Shade said, "This better be important, guys. I was *finally* asleep."

"Son," Monique said as she continued to brush the yard and a half of her hair, "they didn't drag you out just to mess with you."

"Uh-huh," Shade said. "So, let's hear it—how is it I'm jammed up?"

"No one said you *are* jammed up," Francois said. He looked none too thrilled to be out at this hour himself. He was taller than Shade by a few inches and when tired, as now, he slouched. His hair was dark and razor-cut and within a flippant curl or two of being too hip for the D.A.'s office. There was blue stubble on his lean, sanguine face and he wore a plum-colored jogging suit that was unstained by sweat. "We got you out at this hour to tell you that you better watch your step." Francois shoved the eight ball against the far rail and it banked around the table in an ever widening pattern of caroms. "Rene—I heard something today. Then How called a little while ago and we put it together."

Shade stood next to the pool table and caught the eight ball as it died against the rail. He hefted the ball, shifting his head from side to side.

"How much do you know?"

"Rene," How said, "how much do *you* know? Huh? That's the question that's got us out of bed."

With his mother's brushstrokes rhythmically sounding behind him, the green-shaded light above the table shining on his hand, his hand holding the black ball, his face in shadows, he said, "Enough to take care of my ass. It's touching that you guys are concerned, but . . ."

"You ever heard about Captain Bauer and the Carpenter brothers?" Francois asked. "You must've, eh?"

"Sure. I heard it. I think it's true, too."

"Good," Francois said. "You know who his partner was on that?"

"A cop named Delahoussaye, wasn't it?"

"That's what I always heard," How said.

Francois leaned back on the rail, then rubbed his eyes wearily.

"That's right," he said. "Plus Larry Carpenter."

"Larry Carpenter?" Shade said. "Whatta you talkin' about? Larry was one of the dead ones."

"He was the oldest brother. Rene, Larry Carpenter had a bourbon-whipped liver and two daughters and a wife who'd flipped and he'd started a war with Mr. B. that he'd come to realize he just couldn't win. He set his brothers up for Bauer and Delahoussaye to *arrest* them, but, as you know, funny things happen when you're in the dark with Karl Bauer."

Still on her stool, Monique said, "Karl was scary since as long as I recall." She looked like a veteran necromancer, wreathed by smoke from a long brown cigarette. "He's been mean ever since pantyhose ruined finger fuckin'."

"When would that be, Ma?" Shade asked.

"Oh," she said, "a good while." Monique wore a white smock and pink fuzzies on her feet. "That was about when I had Tip."

How Blanchette's pale face flushed, as it did when people he still thought of as "parents" talked bluntly. Monique Blanqui Shade had caused more blushes than Revlon.

"Frankie," How said, "is that why Delahoussaye committed suicide?"

"I'm going to answer that for your benefit, Rene. There was some teamwork involved in Delahoussaye's suicide.

136

Paul Lowell was D.A. way back then, and he told me this: Delahoussaye was talking to somebody in the state attorney's office." Francois then leaned over and punched his index finger at Shade's chest. "You look like the Delahoussaye in this deal, Rene. If it blows up, man, they're going to send your ass down for it."

"Or worse," Shade said.

"That's right."

"And comrade," How said, "there's more news. You know Ralph Duroux from Tecumseh Street? Well, he's got some problems he wants help on. He called me out of bed and tells me Shuggie Zeck had a game knocked over tonight. At a strip joint out there, The Rio, Rio. A man was killed."

Shade groaned and said, "Oh, that sly shitass."

"You been with Shuggie all day, ain't you? It's you and him on this, right?"

"Yeah, it's me and him."

"Watch your ass with him," Francois said.

"I am."

"Did he call you?" Blanchette asked. "I mean, this killing was around eleven or so. He call you?"

"No."

"You're partners and he didn't call you? What's that make you think?"

What it made Shade think was hot things, then cold things, then calm things. He squeezed between his mother and the Dr Pepper cooler and went to the phone. He dialed a number and waited. And waited. After twenty-seven rings he hung up.

He rejoined How and Francois.

"Well, it stinks," he said. "Shuggie's snowin' me, ain't he? It stinks. He's not home, either."

137

How Blanchette was spread out against the pool table, chewing his lips, using his choppers to delicately skin himself.

"Rene," he said, "you want I should come with on this? Huh? Don't trust Shuggie, man. I know him, too, and that's my advice."

"No, man, no," Shade said. "Stay out of it and clean."

Francois said, "Keep me up to date in case I need to do what I can. Rene, tell How what's what and I'll get it from him."

"Sure, counselor," Shade said. "You don't want any calls from me in your phone log."

Francois smiled.

"Damage control," he said.

Shade nodded, then walked over to his mother and pecked her on the cheek.

"Time to be hard-nosed," he said. "Like you raised us."

"Try not to get caught out in the shit trap," Francois said. "It's liable to get deep fast."

"I hear you. I hear you. I'll try to keep the Shade name clean so you can run for mayor someday, *Frankie*."

"Someday might come sooner than you think," Francois said sharply. "If this thing goes awry but awry *correctly*, it could be pretty *damn* soon. Hear me? And if I was ever to be elected, well, it wouldn't be the worst thing that ever happened to you two."

Monique hopped off the stool, her hair hanging down and around her like a witch's cloak, and rapped her hairbrush on Shade's back, and when he turned she pointed the ebony-handled boar bristles at him.

"Listen to your brother," she said. Her arm was fully extended and the brush was aimed between Shade's eyes.

"I wouldn't tell you to squat when you pee or curtsy to hoodlums or kiss any man's ass—but son, I'm askin' you to listen to your brother. It's not too much to ask of you, is it?"

St. Bruno, being north of the French Triangle but south of the Mason-Dixon, below the deep-freeze belt but above the land of tropical ease, was not naturally endowed with beaches. Therefore, north out of town, past two miles of slushy terrain, cinder-block roadhouses, and whitewashed shacks, one had been made. Golden Rule Creek, a sluggish stream, had been diverted into a long shallow trough, surrounded by trucked-in white sand. The place was called Holiday Beach and, for ten bits a head, the citizenry could recline on sand as alluring as any in the Caribbean, there to sip various fruit-based elixirs, eat grilled prawns, and take bold dives into the unfortunately brown lagoon.

Only one road connected Holiday Beach to the highway, and Officer Tommy Mouton used the spotlight on his squad car to find a place where he could safely back off of it and hide.

"That looks okay," he said, spotlighting a fairly flat area between two gullies.

"Sure," Shuggie Zeck said, without bothering to look. "Whatever."

Mouton backed into the spot, then doused the lights. He was hooked on menthol and lit one of a constant chain of Kools.

"After this I'm the iceman, eh?" he asked. "For sure?"

"I said you would be." Shuggie had the sawed-off shotgun resting on his lap. His left hand was swollen from contact with his wife's hard head. His tone of voice was somber. "Quit actin' like you don't believe me. When I say it I mean for you to believe it."

The bright glow of the cigarette lit Mouton's features expressionistically, like a jack-o'-lantern.

"I can use the money," he said. "I really can. My old lady's pregnant again." Mouton considered himself to be a sharply packaged brand of manhood: slim, square-chinned and dusky, with a go-to-hell moustache and razorblade eyes. "So's my girl friend. I can *definitely* use the money." He tossed the butt out the window and immediately lit another. "They cost me, but they're both fun, you know what I mean?"

"No," Shuggie said crisply, "I don't."

"That's too bad," Mouton said. "It's the one thing I agree with the professors and radicals on, you know. Smash monogamy. It's more natural to the human animal to smash monogamy. Smash it into pieces—get it? That's what *they* say. I'm willin' to go that far with the hippies and the eggheads, but no further. Past that point they're full of shit."

Shuggie sat calmly, staring out the window toward the highway, waiting for oncoming headlights. He'd taken a pint of peppermint schnapps from the trunk of his El Dorado, but had yet to break the seal.

"When they come, swing up beside them—fast," Shuggie said. "No cherrytop, no nothin'."

"Gotcha," Mouton responded. "So, Rene Shade ain't got it in him, huh? I always heard he was a tough guy. Like Tip. I know Tip from around The Chalk and Stroke years ago. He's a brute. I always heard Rene was, too, only smaller, weight-wise."

"He's not the right man for this," Shuggie said. "He

might go soft when you least expect it. He ain't got your stones, Tommy."

"Who does?" Mouton smiled. "Some of those hunchbacks maybe do. Hah, hah. It takes a strong spine to lug around a set of . . ."

"Shut up, Tommy. I don't like men who talk about their privates all the time. It's better if it's girls talkin' about a man's rigging, Tommy. When a man does it it's like—'I hear the sizzle, and if you show me the steak I'll belt you.'"

"Wow," Mouton said. "That's pretty harsh." He inhaled some more Kool smoke. "I guess the sixties musta just passed you right by."

For the next several minutes the men sat quietly, watching lightning bugs and listening to tree frogs. The moon was dropping away and stars paling. A pleasant breeze shook the trees and across the beach a cock mistimed sunrise and began crowing prematurely.

"So," Mouton said, "the bottom line is, all these punks have got to go."

Shuggie exhaled wearily. "Tommy, what did I tell you?"

15

There was a mailbox at the curb atop an ornate piece of black, pseudo-French grillwork, and on the side, in fancy script, it said, The Zecks. Up the short driveway from the street was a refurbished house that had once been a duplex of shotgun apartments. Now the place was nicely painted a shiny yellow, and a broad, rounded, black and white awning spread over the two original doors.

Shade parked a ways down the block, then walked along the drive to the house. Despite the unanswered phone call he thought Shuggie might be at home. He didn't see the El Dorado on the street but went on up to the house anyway. On the porch, under the awning, he saw that the inside door was open, so he pulled on the screen, and it was unlatched. He let himself in and found himself to be in a wide parlor that had been made by busting down some walls. All walking in here was done on carpet, and he went quietly into the other rooms.

At the kitchen he smelled alcohol and pie. For some reason he wanted his pistol out, and quickly it was. There

142

was a short counter between the kitchen and dining room and he paused at it.

That's when he heard ice cubes clicking and water dripping. All of the house was in darkness and he was tired enough to suspect himself of hallucinatory vision, but he thought there was someone sitting at the table. The whatever it was he saw seemed to bend forward and make sputtering noises.

Shade crept forward, hand on the wall. Halfway there he happened across the light switch, and flipped it up.

Hedda Zeck sat at the dining table, her face submerged in a clear glass mixing bowl full of ice and water. There were wisps of blood sloshed among the ice cubes. She raised her head, looked blankly at Shade, then said, "I didn't holler cop."

"Jesus," Shade said.

She had Killer Bee–stung lips and her visage had been brutalized into asymmetry. The left side was puffed out to here and the eye on that side would be winking purplish at the world for a while. Finger-sized bruises were imprinted on both cheeks and high on the throat.

"Did you hear me?" she asked.

"God damn, Hedda," Shade said. He holstered his pistol and stepped toward her. "Shuggie whipped you like that?"

She gave no answer but the dropping of her face into the ice bowl. When she pulled up out of the bowl Shade repeated his question. She answered, "Of course not. I bought a case of bad makeup, you dumb fuck." Then she resubmerged, trying to hold down the swelling.

Shade went to the phone and found that the cord had been yanked from the wall. He went back to Hedda, pulled out a chair and sat next to her. When she paused to breathe again, he said, "Want me to run you to St. Joe's?"

"Oh, Rene," she answered and started to weep. She turned to him and he held her. "He was mean, *so* mean. I did something wrong, but he was *so, so*, mean."

During the long, slow courtship of Shuggie and Hedda, Shade had been a fairly constant witness to the proceedings. He'd sat one seat removed in the balcony of The Strand Theater while the lovebirds had experimented with tongues and touches and fingerbanging, and he'd been the fella with the bottle and the weed on the night Shuggie popped her cherry on a picnic table in Frechette Park while he sat at the other end, drinking peach brandy, too close to ignore their sounds, too stoned to want to.

"I didn't think he could do this," Shade said. She held him tightly, water dripping onto his shoulder. "I never would've believed it." He stood and raised her alongside. "Come on, I'm going to run over to St. Joe's. You ought to be checked out."

She pulled loose of him, her head shaking wildly.

"No. No. Huh-uh. He'll kill me. No. Or my dad'll find out and shoot Shuggie." She backed away, hands up. "I did wrong."

"Maybe so," Shade said, "but now you're a victim."

"Well," she said, as if pondering a multiple-choice question, "well, you know, the weak, the *weak* are notorious for bein' victims. There's a chain of events involved."

"Where is that motherfucker now?"

"Uh, well. Well, Rene, I got a friend, a good friend, I *love* her, really. Her name is Wanda. Shuggie's gone to kill her."

"Why?"

"Oh, he thinks she's in with a gang, or whatnot. He thinks they robbed his games, you know?"

"Who is she?"

"Wanda Bouvier, Rene. That's her name."

Hedda began walking toward the couch, walking with the abysmal choreography of a woman who was out on her feet. "She's married to Ronnie Bouvier."

"I get it," Shade said. "I get it now. How do I find her?"

Hedda stumbled over the coffee table, dumping the Frangelico bottle, dessert bowls, and her bridge to the carpet. She sort of drooled down to the couch, a slow caving in.

"I wouldn't tell him," she said with a faint tone of pride. "But I'll tell you, I'll tell you."

═══ **16** ═══

All kinds of bad feelings had huddled around Leon Roe in the lonely darkness of his house and tormented him. He sat on a metal folding chair near the window that faced Wanda's place, peeking out through the curtains. His hair was disheveled from the several times he had grabbed it and jerked his head around, punishing himself. On his lap sat an open bottle of Fighting Cock bourbon, which he usually kept under the kitchen sink and only dusted off when his mother visited. But tonight, feeling sneak-punched by love and hope, he had suckled down a few inches of hundred proof.

A couple of swigs ago he had seen a car leave Wanda's drive with three people in it, and now he tapped the toes of his boots to the floor in a fast upbeat tempo, impatiently waiting to see if anyone else came out. He didn't know if Wanda had been in the car or not, but he didn't think so. As he put the bottle to his lips there were tears in his eyes, for the prettiest girl in Frogtown clearly didn't know or care how much he dug her, *no, more* than dug her, *grooved* on her. All he wanted was to win her heart and take her away from all this and give her nice, soft, silky things to wear and write songs based on her bein' a spike of honeyed sunshine in a lonesome rockabilly boy's life and play with her tits whenever he wanted. But she refused to see this. She didn't see it at all. She was with *them*.

Swig, sniffle, and sigh.

And they were bad.

Leon rose up from his chair and, bottle in hand, went outside. Between the swaying limbs of trees he could see a light on across the street. He went toward it, sidling a bit to the left of straight, unaccustomed as he was to heavy drink. But he felt like a new man, or at least a man, and staggered right up the steps and in the front door.

He knew the layout of the house from visits he'd paid to previous tenants. The rooms had hardwood floors and were sparsely furnished and his footsteps seemed to drum out. He swilled more liquor and dribbled some down his chin and onto the nice shirt that was already stained by blood, so what the hell.

A narrow hallway led past the john and that's where he heard her. She was in there tootin' and turnin' pages.

The door was open a crack and there she sat on the commode looking at the fashion pictures in an old water-stained *Cosmo*.

He shoved the door open and her eyes turned to him, and with the Fighting Cock in his hand he pointed at her. He said, "Wanda, you put me face-to-face with death tonight. You put me in a horrible place." He burped and wobbled. "My quick thinkin' saved *you*. For the moment."

"Is that so?" Wanda said. "By the time I wipe my ass you better have done some more quick thinkin', Leon. *Boy.*"

Instinctively courteous, Leon turned his back and listened to the toilet paper roll on the spindle. Then, after the flush, he said, "Shuggie Zeck is gonna kill you deader'n Elvis."

"What?" she said. She squeezed past him and walked toward the kitchen, her face hot and her step panicky. "Leon, why would he . . ."

"Because you're guilty." She stood by the wall and he sat at the table. He shoved empty cans off the tabletop, pinging them to the floor, and set the bottle down. "That's a plain, plain fact, Wanda. You're guilty as hell." He stared at her feet, chin on his chest. "But I ain't givin' up on you yet. Not just yet."

Wanda went to the sink and turned on the cold water. She held her head under the tap trying to cool her brain, for cool thinking was called for here. When her head was thoroughly soaked she stood erect and swept her red hair straight up and back, using her fingers as a comb, and fashioned a dripping, jumbo pompadour.

Then she sat at the table, and said, "You better tell me all about it."

The Wing was driving slowly and hee-hawing in the car toward Holiday Beach. Though the turnoff was clearly marked they'd missed it twice. Dean Pugh drove, Cecil Byrne rode shotgun and Emil Jadick sat in the back. They were riding high, feeling strong, frequently comparing themselves to fantastic miscreants of the past. Several tortured parallels had been drawn between themselves and

The James Gang, Dillinger, Lieutenant Calley, E. F. Hutton and Al Capone.

When Pugh turned down the road to the beach he punched the lights off. He hunched toward the windshield, following the road as nearly as he could.

"You know," he said, "I'm glad we're flippin' off the mob here. In a special sort of way it makes me feel good, flippin' off the mob."

"This is a mob," Jadick said, "but not the dago mob."

"This is a peckerwood mob," Dean said, "but it *is* a mob."

"Sure it's a mob," Jadick said. "But flippin' off the dago mob is where we'll come into the real, *real* money."

"I always stood aside from them," Cecil offered. "The Mafia, I mean."

Jadick made a sarcastic bodily sound.

"Fuck the Mafia," he said. "The Mafia is just all these short tubby greasers who wouldn't last a week on The Yard if you didn't know their friends on the outside would kill your whole family."

"I was in Marion when Roy-Roy Drucci was," Dean said. "He was only about yea tall and plump, and one time this big nigger named Blue went after him." Dean shook his head. "Roy-Roy chopped big bad Blue down like he was a weed, man. Took a wood chisel to his head, skinned him like a turnip. Sort of awesome, really."

"All right, all right," Jadick said tartly. "I didn't mean none of them was rough, just in general."

Pugh put on the brakes. He pointed down the road a ways, and said, "Is that the lights? Is that it?"

And they all leaned forward and peered out the windshield and something came roaring up beside them.

The squad car was all smoked up when Officer Tommy Mouton said, "Hey, look."

"See lights?" Shuggie asked.

"No, but there's a dark shape on the road, movin' slow this way."

"Lock and load," Shuggie said. "We own 'em."

The slow-moving shape was opaque and humped, grumbling on the gravel. Despite the snitching glow of moonlight, the dark car felt its way down the road, right past the black and white. When it was but a few lengths beyond the ambush, Shuggie said, "Let's straighten 'em out," and Mouton fired the engine and whipped up alongside The Wingmen. When Shuggie was abreast of Pugh and Byrne, Mouton flashed the spotlight in their faces, and their expressions of surprise were superb, authentically loose-jawed with eyes stunned wide, and fatal, for that long elastic second of shock allowed Shuggie to aim.

By no design other than sheer opportunity, Shuggie saved both Pugh and Byrne from a period of bereavement, for he saw to it that they died together. With just one pull on the twin-triggered blaster he shredded them in tandem, the spotlight illuming their corporeal dispersal against the dash and windshield. And now, rudderless, The Wing mobile oozed off the graveled road and went nose-down in a shallow gully, slamming the grill against a ripple of earth.

The jolt hurled Jadick against the front seat, pounding the air from his lungs. Without time for a good breath, he acted. He climbed wheezing over the seat, sliding down on the fabric chummed with his gang. There was stench from sphincter release and blood and it was on his arms and he opened the door on the driver's side and shoved

150

Dean Pugh from the car and the body flopped under the wheel, but Jadick slammed the shifter to R and backed over it and up the gully.

The spotlight was swinging around as the squad car pulled a U-turn and this soured any chance for secrecy as it beamed on Jadick. He flipped on his own headlights but couldn't see through the crimson muck on the windshield so he wiped a peephole clear and tromped the gas. The shotgun sounded again and metal tore, but the only hope was flight.

The road was fairly straight and Jadick took it fast, grinding the gravel beneath his wheels, billowing a dust trail. Where the road met the highway there was an antique store with a streetlight near it and Jadick swung wide through the parking lot, beneath the light, and he saw Cecil Byrne in a wad on the floorboard, his head a frayed mop, and a glance in the rearview told him that his current problems drove a St. Bruno police car. And he slid back onto the two-way blacktop and screamed a great, thick-necked, tendon-stretching cry, for he instantly understood just how potent Mr. Beaurain's "protection" was in this chitlin' city.

He picked up Pugh's pistol from the seat beside him and sent a forlorn shot in the other direction.

Foot to floorboard he raced toward town, recognizing all too clearly, but not at all sadly, that he was in yet another of those life crises where the odds for success were the ubiquitous slim and none.

When he was a few hundred yards from the turnoff to Wanda's the rear window shattered. Much to his own surprise he freaked at this, and warm piss ran down his leg.

They were on him. Aiming, he could see. Ready to shred the final Wingman, and he leaned hard on the steering wheel and flew the car off the low bank of the road, and into the bayou.

He bailed out as the car sank to its wheels, for the water here was not deep, and the squad car squealed to a stop. As the spotlight spun on its swivel and beamed on the wet surface, he submerged.

And with each underwater stroke there was a chant in his brain. It went—Set up. Set up. Set up.

══**17**══

Shade was rediscovering all sorts of old skills this night, and as he crept along the narrow walk that ran behind Wanda's house to the back porch he utilized the style of stealth that he'd learned at age twelve when it came to his attention that Connie Pelligrini's knockout momma liked to take her evening bath with the curtains parted in hopes of a breeze. He edged along the brick walkway, inches from the bayou, then quietly went up the steps to the porch. At window height he paused and looked into the kitchen. There was a man in rustic finery and snakeskin boots bent over the sink, retching. An open suitcase sat on the table and every few seconds the bricktop beauty came whirling over to it and stuffed something in.

Despite the myriad night sounds Shade could hear Wanda saying "Oh, no," with every trip to the suitcase, and the retching man came across loud and clear. Shade was waiting to check for more people in the house before making an entry, and he had leaned against the porch door, settling in, when a splash sounded behind him. Then dripping sounds. He heard a breath, and when he turned toward it he looked down a pistol barrel that was backed up by a stocky, swamp-scented creature who said, "One of Mr. B.'s boys, I presume."

"Me? No, no."

"No, no?" Jadick patted Shade down and removed the pistol from his belt holster. "These things are dangerous. You a hitter for Mr. B., huh?"

"No," Shade said. "Ronnie, man. Don't bust that cap on me, man. Come on, I'm a friend of Ronnie's."

Jadick pushed the barrel against Shade's nose.

"A friend, huh? That's interesting."

Mud and leaves and mossy hairs were stuck on Jadick. His eyes seemed to be glowing spots in a bucket of primordial ooze.

"Up the stairs," he said. "In we go."

Shade opened the screen door and stepped onto the porch. A pistol bumped against the back of his head. At the kitchen door he was belted on the neck, then shoved to the floor. As he skidded across the linoleum, Jadick said, "Set another plate, pun-kin. We got company."

Wanda was frozen, bent over the suitcase, her lower lip covering the upper, a long black dress dangling from her hand.

"What's that?" Jadick asked, waving pistols in both hands.

"Oh, man, it's my good dress."

"Not that. The suitcase. What's with the suitcase?"

"I'm packin', Emil."

"So I see." He gestured at Shade. "I don't know who this guy is, but he was scopin' you through the window. I don't know who the other guy is, either, but I'm pretty sure you'll have an explanation."

Wanda turned and dropped the dress into the suitcase.

She swept her hands back and across her jumbo pompadour, looking like a very showy juvenile delinquent from a gone era.

"Oh, Emil. Emil. I got scared. Man, I just started to shake, I didn't know what to think."

Jadick walked past Shade and over to the counter. He plugged the deep-fat fryer into the wall socket. "I'm hungry," he said. "I can't wait. You southern coozes, you don't think it's food if it ain't fried, do you? Huh? Travel has broadened me." As he walked past Shade again he bashed him above the eye.

Shade felt the skin part, as the barrel broke open an old boxing scar. Instinctively he reached out, only to be hit on the ear. He fell dizzily back against the wall. Shade tried to focus his eyes, but the right orb was awash in his own blood. The eyeball seemed to slide. This was an old ring sensation, partial blindness was, and the haunted rules of the past came pointlessly to mind: get on one knee; take an eight count; cover up. Shade slumped sideways.

"Something about him unsettles me," Jadick said. He then gestured at Leon who was curled over the sink. "Hey, you. Yeah, you. Get on the floor with Droopy, here." When Leon had obeyed and sat beside Shade, Jadick said, "So, pun-kin, what *was* it that got you so scared?"

"I realized it was true," she said. She shrugged her shoulders slowly and looked down. "I loved *you*, man. I loved you more than Ronnie, and like the thought scared me."

"Aw, Wanda," Jadick said wistfully, "I know some things about *love*, and what you did to me ain't it." He shook his head, mud clumps and twigs falling from his hair. "It ain't even close. You set me up."

"What? No, man!"

"Sure you did. Dean and Cecil are dead now." He nodded at her several times. "That part of your plan worked
fine."

"I can't believe this," Wanda said.

"You can't believe I ain't dead is what you mean." He
swiveled and aimed pistols at both of the men on the
floor. "So, which one of these guys is your boyfriend?"

"You're my boyfriend."

"No. You're a tramp. You set me up."

Wanda's fingers pulled her T-shirt taut, and she turned
partly sideways, and breathed very deeply.

"You got a stigma in your mind on me, Emil. I never set
you up."

The fryer began to give off faint simmering sounds in
the background.

"I was open with you, Wanda. I was revealing of myself.
You've come to sort of know me, ain't you? That's what
you used to set me up."

Dizzy on the floor, Shade put his palms to the linoleum
to steady himself. Jadick's blows reverberated through his
head, causing his thoughts to meander. He closed his
right eye and focused with the left, gaining a lopsided
view of things. The man next to him stank of bourbon-
based vomit, and on the counter grease sizzled, and standing in a shadow the bricktop beauty was engaged in a
menacing minuet with what appeared to be the Missing
Link.

Jadick said, "Get out some eggs and cornmeal, Miz
Bouvier."

"Huh?"

"Eggs and cornmeal, pun-kin. I want that golden bat-
ter. It's the truth I'm after, and I'm gonna fry your fingers
to get it out of you."

The kitchen was lit by a single bare light bulb. Shade felt suddenly alert as he watched what was happening in the shadows around the edges of the room. Thus lit, the whole room, and every gesture made in it, had a quality of the surreal.

Wanda stepped backward into the light. The pink drained from her face. Her hands came up to her chest, palms out.

"Man, you're serious." She breathed hard and fast. "You'll kill me, won't you?"

"You know I would," Jadick said. "That's why you were packin'."

"Oh, man. I didn't cross you."

Leon Roe had puked himself nearly sober. He squatted on the floor, his legs crossed beneath him, his shirtfront soiled a couple of different ways. In his head one of his dreams was being run. Leon's secret dream was the lurid, darkly lit one, wherein a decent but necessarily dangerous lad had lived the sordid, stray tom life, being no better than he oughta be and often worse, especially where heart-breaking was concerned, until his prowling led him to the back door of an ivory-skinned, clear-eyed earth angel and he unexpectedly succumbed to love and reformation. In the third reel of this tear-drizzler the ex-scoundrel was ratpacked by circumstances and forced to employ various skills from his unsavory past to safeguard the fair lady, her crippled brother, and, in some versions, The American Way itself.

With this dream playing continuously in his mind, Leon began to conjure solutions to the problems of the prettiest girl in Frogtown.

Across the room, Jadick stood before the open door-way of the refrigerator. He turned and shoved a carton of eggs down the counter. He reached to the telephone that hung nearby, and tore it from the wall.

"No help from that quarter," he said, as the phone slammed to the floor. "Get an egg in your hand."

Tears were thinly pouring from Wanda's eyes, and tears were strange to her, but she opened the carton and extracted an egg. It was a brown-shelled egg and she held it in her fist, her face down.

"Squeeze," Jadick said.

As she squeezed the egg and the yolk gooed between her clenched fingers, Wanda reached the last ditch and said, "Emil, don't hurt me—I'm with child."

"You're what?"

"I'm carryin' your baby, man. I'm pregnant by you."

"How could you know that?" Jadick's head shook sternly. "I only been humpin' you a week, how would you know you're knocked up?"

Wanda brought both hands to her lower stomach and clasped them, yolk and shells falling to the floor.

"A woman can tell these things. Emil, a woman just *knows* sometimes. I felt it when you fucked me."

"Let me feel of it," Jadick said. He advanced on her and touched the barrels of both pistols to her tummy. "That's where the little critter is?" he asked.

"I know it is," she said. "I know it is."

"Huh," he said, then slammed a pistol butt to her belly. As she slumped to her knees, he said, "Welcome to Daddy's world."

Reviving from his tearjerker dream, Leon embarked on an act of solo bravado, and sprang forward and grabbed Jadick at the knees and pulled him to the floor. Jadick banged him on the head with the pistol then rolled away from him.

Then he shot the rockabilly boy in the stomach.

And Wanda reacted despite the pain in her gut, and raised up and swept the hissing fat fryer off of the counter and onto Emil's mid-section.

The pain caused The Wingman to drop both pistols and scream, his eyes rolling back in his head.

Wanda stood, transfixed by the steaming man below her, and the gut-shot man across the floor.

Shade knew good fortune when he saw it and rose to his feet, then retrieved his pistol. Jadick was going into shock, his voice locked in a steady, monotonous, "Uhhhh . . ." A pool of grease smoldered on and around Jadick's legs and hands. Burning flesh scented the room.

Shade straddled Jadick's shoulders, wiping the blood back from his own eyes. He leaned over the prone man, the man he'd been told to hit, cocked his pistol, put the muzzle near the forehead, then, for reasons he would long wonder about, he did not shoot. He eased the hammer down, and stepped back.

"Oh, man," Wanda shrieked. "Who are *you*? Do I know you, man? Oh, man, tell me, who the fuck are *you*?"

His thoughts were still fuzzy around the edges, but Shade said, "As much good luck as you could ask for." He gestured at the two men on the floor.

"They might make it. Help me get them to the car."

But Wanda Bone Bouvier just stood there, stalled by the crimson events, until Shade spun her about and kicked her hard on the ass, the jolt bouncing her against the kitchen sink.

"Help me get them to the car!"

18

"I think Leon's dead," Wanda Bone Bouvier said from the backseat. She sat between the two wounded men, smeared with gore from fingertips to forehead. "Oh, man, he's dead."

Shade was driving, trying to see through the film of his own blood running into his right eye, his right hand held to the rip in his brow, attempting to divert the flow.

"Which one's Leon?"

"The boy. Man," she said, her voice hitting awkward, brittle notes, "Leon is the boy."

Jadick was in shock, his hands blistered rare, eyes rolling in his head.

"We'll be at St. Joe's in a minute," Shade said. Pain and blood and punishment; he knew these things, he had no confusion when confronted with them. "I'm a cop," he said, "in case you're too fuckin' stupid to know that."

"Oh, man, my life has turned out just like Momma said it would—a screamin' mess of shit. She said that to me, way back in time."

That's when the cherrytop appeared in the rearview

mirror, the light revolving, stabbing beams of red into the car. He watched the redness infuse Wanda's face, which had suddenly become still.

"Zeck," he said under his breath, certain somehow that Shuggie was behind him now. "Mouton."

Leon the dead boy lay with his head on Wanda's shoulder. She moved him away and turned to look out the rear window.

"Oh, man, it's him—it's Shuggie Zeck!" Her voice came out in a flat whine. "Oh, man, oh, man, oh, man."

Shade punched the gas pedal and the blue Nova shot forward. The wheels skimmed over the hard cobblestone street, sounding like a jet distant in the clouds. He turned hard left up Voltaire Street.

Wanda lurched forward and clutched at his shoulder blades, her fingernails biting in.

"You can't give me up to Shuggie, man. You can't do that! He'll turn me inside out!" That close she had a strong metallic odor of blood and fear-laced sweat and some lingering jasminy perfume. "You gotta promise! You gotta—"

"Shut up!" He stole a look into the rearview mirror. "Sit back and keep your fucking head down."

His mind shifted into another gear where action came independent of precise thought. He floated the car over a blacktopped rise in the road, then turned into a used-car lot, cutting toward the alley. It was Laughlin's Car Lot. A part of the neighborhood. He and Shuggie, here at night after seeing *Love Me Tender* at The Strand, hair slicked into a duckass, and they'd been jamming an unwound wire hanger through the window seal of a highly coveted '57 Chevy, yearning to cruise the backroads with the wind in their hair, when Laughlin himself had fired a shot

161

over their heads, and strong young legs had carried them to safety. And Shade's thoughts that night and this had centered on the issue of bad companions, bad choices, and questionable self. To be alive, alive to the bone, is to make mistakes, but to stay alive you must learn from them. Then and now.

Shade's Nova was small and light and overhorsed and it maneuvered easily through the maze of parked cars. Wanda's sobs and invitations to the deity to save her were constant background noise. He pulled onto Second Street, going the opposite way, and her voice pitched higher as they jolted over the curb. The patrol car was still on him, right there, behind by a few lengths. St. Joe's Hospital was in sight, a tall pale stone building that rose into view just beyond the dark brick of St. Peter's.

Would they dare make a hit in front of the hospital?

From the backseat Wanda wailed, "Those cops will blow me away! Look, look, you can't—"

"Shut up!"

Shade shook the steering wheel, surprised by the frantic heat of his own voice.

The tires squealed musically as he swerved around a corner on Second Street. The sky was lightening and there was some traffic farther up the street. The street itself, with its bumps and holes, formed a useless kind of jolting litany. Memory has a rhythm all its own, and Shade's lips moved soundlessly as his mind flashed back on the mournful quality of a certain rainy afternoon when they'd fought on a sandbar below the highway bridge, but he couldn't remember why . . . and the warm expansiveness of a spring evening when their feet clapped down this street, this very street, outrunning Father Geoghegan who'd made an irresistible target for their peashooters.

Memories came one after another, like the ruby beads on his rosary which he'd once known how to use. And all the time Shade could hear a bubbling, gurgling sound from the wounded man, Jadick, in the backseat, like a fish drowning in air.

There was a shortcut through the church parking lot that he'd used all his life, especially after having learned to drive. By following it youths could fashion a circular racing track without resorting to an actual road. Many scores had been settled here and many grudges born.

Shade wheeled into the church parking lot, instinctively taking the path he'd used so many times before. He swung past the jungle gyms and the swings with crooked seats. He raced toward the alley behind the dumpster, between the church and rectory, hoping to put distance between himself and the pursuing red light. He was well into the alley when he saw that a line of cement posts now barricaded the passageway. For a brief moment the posts seemed unreal to Shade, they didn't belong to the landscape that he knew and his mind rebelled. The loud scream of his brakes brought him to. The Nova fishtailed as it came to a halt.

Then he remembered having heard that Monsignor Escalera had erected the barrier a year ago to stop the traditional youth races.

The patrol car was squeezing down the alleyway behind them. Shade opened the door and got out. He shoved the seat forward. "Beat it!" He pulled Wanda over Jadick, and out of the car. "Find a place to hide," he said, but Wanda froze at his side, staring dumbly at the dark windshield of the St. Bruno patrol car. "Hide yourself in the goddamned church," he said harshly, and her legs began moving away from the red light.

163

When the patrol car came to a halt Shuggie Zeck came springing out from the passenger side. Shade watched Zeck lumber up the church steps. Shade pulled his pistol and held it down near his thigh. He glanced into his car at Jadick, who still breathed though he might have preferred to be dead. The patrol car moved cautiously up to the rear bumper of the Nova. Shade approached the driver. A strange veil of calm had descended over him.

"You're Mouton, right?" he said loudly. "I been lookin' for you."

Officer Tommy Mouton stepped out of the dark cab of the patrol car. He did not wear a hat and his hand rested on the butt of his pistol.

He said, "*You* been lookin' for *me*?"

"Yeah," Shade said. "I was hopin' to find you before it was too late." Shade planted his pistol inside of his waistband, then swept one hand over his bloody brow. "I got the son of a bitch. Come on, he's in the car."

There were a few cars pulling into the parking lot slightly in advance of the early mass, and Shade was gambling that Tommy Mouton wouldn't back-shoot him when visible to them. At the Nova, Shade placed both hands on the window and looked into the backseat.

"I'd like to bust about three caps in his head right now, but Mr. B. doesn't want it that way."

Mouton looked in on the backseat, took in Leon's body and Jadick. He said, "Who's the other guy? There's only supposed to be one more."

"He was with them and he got in the way."

Mouton stepped back and nodded slowly. "You *are* a brute."

Shade kept his head down and said, "Mr. B. wants him alive. There was an inside man on this, and he wants to

164

find out for sure who put the finger on the games."

"The *girl* did that," Mouton said, "and that's why the girl and this cat have to go."

"Shuggie tell you that?" Shade said swiftly. "I bet he did. Sure he did. *Shuggie* set the games up, sport. That's why he don't want nobody livin' through this but *him*. He knows Mr. B.'s smart."

Mouton said, "Are you shittin' me? I think you're shittin' me."

"Christ, why do you think he cut me out of this?" Shade said.

Mouton eyed him nervously. "I don't know," he said, "I don't know about this."

"Shit you don't know fills libraries, Mouton," Shade said. "I just came from Beaurain's this morning. You wanta be on the right side of the man, you listen to me. You wanta be on the wrong side of the man, you just keep thinkin' you're smart."

"You don't sound like you're shittin' me."

"I'm not," Shade said, taking a step back from the car. "Get the burned guy here over to the hospital quick. I'm gonna get in there after Shuggie before he has time to cap his secret squeeze."

"This ain't what Shuggie said."

"I'm sure it ain't," Shade said. "Who do you think woulda been the last guy he had to waste, ya dumb fuck? He's got you in way deep now."

Mouton's sharp presence seemed to dull upon hearing this, his feet shifted uncertainly.

"I wanna be on Mr. B.'s good side," he said.

"Smart," Shade answered, then turned his back on Mouton, walked up the alley and into the church.

A weak broth of light fell through the vaulted windows

of St. Peter's and spilled across the dark tiled floor. Shade edged along the near wall, then stood quietly. He took a step and his shoe squeaked, the sound echoing up to the Gothic ceiling. A permanent smell of incense wafted from the walls and pews, a sensual link to an older sensibility. A couple of tapers burned in front of an icon of the Virgin, the flames flickering with the currents of air. Perhaps some old woman had been here before dawn, or maybe even Wanda Bouvier had paused in her haste to light a candle before she hid.

Suddenly Shuggie was right beside him, loosely holding the sawed-off. He'd been standing in the shadow. Shuggie nodded at him knowingly.

"She's a bad cookie, Rene, we both know that." Car doors slammed outside the building, the sound muffled through the brick walls. "She's *very* bad cookies now. She's gotta go. Understand? I don't want to have to kill you, but I will if you push it. This comes from high up."

Shade smiled at him then.

"Don't count on it," he said.

"Rene, you're buckin' the big boys on this. You ain't slappin' the shit outta some coonass like Gillette. This is Mr. B. You're gonna get hurt bad."

Shade held his hands spread wide, laid his head onto one shoulder, smiling, and said, "Ain't that the point?"

"Jerk."

"Where is she?"

Shuggie shrugged. "Somewhere in here. I laid on the floor and looked under the pews. I can't see her."

Shade said, "You don't want to kill a cop, Shuggie. I'll find her."

Shuggie snorted at him and the sound expanded with resonance.

"Be smart," he said.

"Be smart? Smart like you?" Shade punched a forefinger at Shuggie's chest. "I saw what you did to Hedda. I was over there. Yeah. You fuckin' punk. *I ain't Hedda.*" Shade grasped but did not pull the pistol in his waistband. Shuggie blanched. He looked away. His mouth opened wide and he rocked his head back on his neck.

"I didn't want to do that. I wish I didn't, but I had to. Her talkin' was out of control."

Shade spit onto Shuggie's pant leg. "Take off, sport. Just go. I wanta see that fat ass of yours framed in that doorway, going out."

Shuggie took a few paces backward. The shotgun was aimed down and it wavered in his hand.

"I don't know if you can back that shit up, Rene. I could kill you."

"You reckon?" Shade answered.

"Well," Shuggie said, smiling almost wistfully. "We always wondered about this, ain't we?"

Shade nodded and turned sideways to Shuggie.

"I guess so."

They stared from shadow to shadow, then Shuggie turned away.

"Fuck this. I'm goin'. We can take care of her anytime."

As Shuggie walked away, Shade sat on the last pew and used the polished wood seatback for a gun rest. He cocked his pistol and took aim at the center of Shuggie's back.

"I know you're going to go for it, Shuggie."

"You think I'm a fool? I heard that pistol cock."

"I think you're gonna go for it, Shug," Shade said and put both hands onto his pistol. "Whatever that means."

Shuggie's laughter resounded throughout the cavernous

room and Shade watched with a sense of incredulity as Shuggie walked to the door and out.

For a moment Shade just sat there breathing deeply, his hands clenching.

From beneath the altar came a low, scuffling noise. Then he heard Wanda's voice as she said, "Oh, man—what now?"

He heard the explosion then, a single shot fired in the alley. He went quickly to the door and cracked it open, pistol at the ready, then he swung the door wide and stepped out, looking down on Shuggie. There below him, belly to the asphalt, Zeck lay already dead, a fist-sized piece of his skull swinging open as if hinged, a rush of blood and brains running down his back.

Officer Tommy Mouton stood a few feet away. He jerked his thumb to his chest, his face clutched in a terrible sneer.

"*I'm* the iceman, now," he said. "Put me right with Mr. B., Shade, don't you take credit for it. Don't try that. *I'm* the iceman now."

Shade was choking on his own breath. He raised his face straight up, and there, at a dominating height above them all, he saw the first light of the new day glinting from the cross atop the steeple. And as he followed the trajectory from that shimmering point to the bloody asphalt below, it seemed that Shuggie had been spit from precisely there, to come to rest, inevitably, just like this.

And in the next instant Wanda Bone Bouvier, bloodstained and otherwise soiled, pulled at his shoulders, gasped at the body, and said, "Oh, thank you, Jesus, just this once."